There is Life After

PUSHED BACK TO STRENGTH

Kay B. Ruffin

Acknowledgment

First and foremost, I want to acknowledge my God, Jehovah, because without Him, there would be no book or me. I give thanks to him for placing the dream of becoming a writer in my heart and for his desire to follow that dream. I give thanks to him for showing me my purpose and for giving me the ability to execute that purpose.

I want to give a special thanks to my dear friend, Lucille Gregg, for listening to me talk about my desire to become a published author over 35 years ago. She not only listened to me, but she heard me. I thank her for consistently encouraging me to go for my dream. Her faith in me gave me the strength that I needed to make my dream come true.

A heartfelt thanks to my niece, Akiyah Carey, and to my sister-in-law, Margaret Wright, for taking the time to read my very first draft in its roughest form and for letting me know I had something worth completing. Their feedback was priceless.

Many thanks to my wonderful family, Chevonne, Marcus, and Paul Byas, for all their unrelenting support and encouragement; this is for them. A special thanks to my brother Ronald Ruffin and my niece Teri Montgomery for all their advice and support.

Dedication

I dedicate this book to my children; Chevonne and Marcus Byas. Who has always supported and encouraged me to fulfill my dream of becoming an author. And to my granddaughters, Nuriyah and Nasirah, and to all my other grands who will come behind them.

This is for you and for all that you dare dream, with my unconditional love.

About the Author

Kay B. Ruffin is a retired mother of two and has two precious granddaughters. After experiencing the loss of her mother at a young age, her family means everything to her.

In addition to spending quality time with her family, her mission was to complete her debut novel "There is Life After" in her retirement. A goal which she has accomplished. She is now working towards her second novel which will precede the events in her first novel. Although the second story will take on a life of its own, it will describe what led up to the events in the prior novel.

Kay B. has always been a daydreamer. From a very young age, she lived in her head, reinventing the stories she had read while imagining that she was somewhere else. It has been her lifelong dream to become an author. At the age of thirteen, after completing an essay for an English class, she knew then that she wanted to write professionally.

As a child she always had a love for reading. Her love for reading, her vivid imagination and her life experiences all went into writing her debut novel.

In college, she majored in early childhood education, however it was her English creative writing courses that she excelled in. Several years later, after going through her own challenges and personal ups and downs, she began journaling. Journaling allowed her to put some of her challenges into words.

She signed up for creative writing classes at the Gotham Writer's Workshop. In the workshop, she wrote and shared her short stories with others in the group. One of her short stories, along with some of her journal entries, went into creating her debut novel. She also attended a two-day conference at the International Women's Writing Guild for two consecutive years, where she met with various literacy agents who reviewed her book proposal and gave her valuable feedback and encouragement. From there, she continued developing her story.

Through her story "There is Life After," she hopes that people will find comfort in knowing that they can move forward after facing some of life's most difficult challenges. She also wants to bring awareness to the mental health crisis that many are facing today. Especially women who are struggling to raise their families despite depression or other crises that plague families today.

The message that she hopes to convey to her readers is that pulling together as a family, either biological family or close-knit friends, will ultimately help make their struggle easier and worthwhile.

Table of Context

Chapter One
Zach's Departure

This somber morning, as expected, the Taylor's house was unusually quiet. It was as if everyone in the house was in a trance, all except for Granny, who, as usual, was all reared up and ready to go. Granny was always full of energy, especially when it came to taking care of business.

"Let's get a move-on, Shania; the limo's outside. They're not going to wait all day," Granny said to Shania, trying to bring full energy into her voice.

"They'll wait, Granny; they're used to folks being late for these things," Shania answered as she walked down the stairs in her house, almost in a trance. "Is everyone ready?" she asked. Her eyes were puffy, and her voice was raspy due to crying all night.

"Yes, everyone's ready; we're waiting on you. We still have to swing by and pick up Gary," answered Granny. Her heart ached for Shania. "Let's get this over with," Shania heaved a deep sigh of grief and said as she stepped onto her front porch. Deep down, she knew that getting over it was not going to be easy. She had no idea how long it would take her to accept reality. She stopped for a moment and looked up at the sky as her family piled into the limousine.

"When I said 'until death do us part,' Zach, this was not what I had in mind," she said to herself as tears trickled down her cheeks. She wanted to yell at the top of her lungs. She began to shiver. Her grief was taking a toll on her body and soul. Nevertheless, she pulled her black wrap tightly around her shoulders and walked towards the waiting limo. She never imagined she would be going to her husband's funeral at this stage of their lives.

She was so deep into her grief that she didn't even notice the car pulling out or the fact that it had stopped until she felt the warmth of her Uncle Gary's body as he slipped into the seat next to her. Everyone was quiet; the limo itself smelled like death.

Shania didn't have any experience with planning a funeral, so Granny and Zach's mother, Ella, had taken care of most of the arrangements. The only thing that Shania had to do was to pick out Zach's suit. She did, however, insist that Zach's service not be held in a church. Ella wasn't too happy about that because she wanted his service to be held at her church. Shania knew that Zach wasn't a religious man and would have thought it hypocritical to have his service there. Shania could hear him objecting now. There were a few times when she had managed to drag him to church, but he always complained, saying he felt like a hypocrite. She wasn't going to let him spend the rest of his eternity feeling that way. So, after some coaching from Granny, Ella agreed to have the service at the Mountain Top Funeral Home in southeast Atlanta.

Ella had raised her family in the Church of God in Christ (COGIC), which is the largest Pentecostal-Holiness Christian denomination in the

US, with the majority of members being African American. Shania was raised in the Baptist Church.

Her grandmother was a long-time member of the famous Ebenezer Baptist Church in Atlanta, where Martin Luther King, Jr., once preached. Baptist Churches are very popular in the South, with a large majority being African American as well. Although Baptists tend to be more conservative than other Christian denominations, they are not as strict as COGIC. Zach was turned off by religion mainly because of COGIC's very strict doctrines.

As the family entered the chapel in the funeral home, Shania looked around. All their family members and friends were there to pay their respects. Shania forced a smile to greet them, although her heart was weeping. At the back of the chapel, she noticed a woman who looked vaguely familiar. She figured it was probably a friend of Zach's that she'd met before.

After everyone was seated, the Funeral Director said a few words of comfort, followed by a brief prayer. Reverend Butler from Ella's church gave a heartfelt eulogy, after which friends and family were invited up to the podium one by one to share their fond memories of Zach and express their condolences to the grieving family. The service ended with a song and a prayer.

After the service, family and close friends headed to the cemetery for the interment. Shania was dreading it but knew there was no getting out of it; it was inevitable, and no matter how much she wanted to, there was no point in prolonging it. Once everyone arrived at the burial plot,

Reverend Butler asked them to hold hands before he led them in prayer. He then asked the immediate family to approach the casket and pay their respects to the deceased. He handed each of them a white rose to place on Zach's coffin. It was customary for Shania and Zach's mother to be the first to place their roses.

Shania began to shake as she walked towards the casket, and their whole life together flashed in the back of her mind. Everyone thought she was going to drop the rose as her hands trembled so intensely. Her eldest son Trey helped to steady her as she placed the rose on Zach's coffin before walking away. When it came time to lower the casket to the ground, Shania turned away. Her heart couldn't take it. It was already hard enough to do all of this; watching him go like that was too much. Although she couldn't bear to watch Zach being lowered to the ground, it tore at her heart as she heard her daughter Zaria and her youngest son Zane crying as they watched. She wasn't prepared to do life without Zach, and no matter how much she wanted to avoid addressing the elephant, she would have to do it all by herself now.

The crushing weight of reality shook her. It took all she had to hold herself together when she heard Zach's mother cry, "Why, Zach? Why did you leave us?" This was a question Shania had asked a hundred times. She thought as she walked towards the waiting limo one last time.

In the days leading up to the service, Shania managed to avoid most of her friends and relatives as they stopped by the house to extend their condolences or to drop off a dish for the family. She loved her family and friends, and she loved to spend time with them. However, the pain of losing her other half was so intense that she was blinded by her suffering.

She remained holed up in her guest room, trying to avoid everyone as much as she could. Right now, she does not have the strength to be in her bedroom. Every time she would think of going there, the memory of the lifeless body of her husband would come back to haunt her. Now, on the ride back to her home, she feared that she would have to face everyone as they stopped by the house for the repast.

"Granny, I wish you hadn't invited everyone to the house. How am I supposed to face all these people?" Shania cried as the limo drove them back to her house.

"You know it's customary for folks to get together after a funeral, Shania. If you'd let us have it in a church, then we could've had the repast there. Besides, who's gonna eat all that food people brought over to the house?" Granny tried to talk some sense into her. She knew Shania was in no state to think clearly.

"I know, Granny, but I don't know if I can handle being around anyone," Shania expressed her fears that were engulfing her whole body.

"You're doing just fine baby. I'm here to help you through this." Granny said as she reached over and grasped her hand. She squeezed it gently to reassure Shania that she was there with her.

"I know you are, Granny," she whispered. "But you don't understand," Shania said, thinking no one could possibly understand her shame. Zach's death had given her a lot to think about, and she couldn't stop thinking about where she went wrong.

"No one's blaming you, Shania," Granny once again reassured her.

Shania didn't answer. She leaned her head back on the headrest as she wondered how Granny always knew what she was thinking and how she always had just the right words to say to her. She closed her eyes for the remainder of the drive and wondered if there was something she could have done to prevent this, and that was all she had been thinking about these past couple of days. She didn't understand why she hadn't seen this coming. She kept thinking about how distant she and Zach had become in the past year and if she should have done things differently.

If only she could go back in time and fix everything that had gone wrong, Zach would be here with them, her kids would still have a father, and she would still have a husband. This all seemed like a bad dream, and she could not wake up. The heaviness she felt in her chest wouldn't go away. The pain was almost too much for her to bear, but somehow, she knew that she had to hold on for her children's sake. The world had come crumbling down to her feet, yet she had to stand strong.

Back at the house, Shania tried her best to be cordial to the guests as they stopped by for the repast. But after a while, it became tedious, and it was just too much for her, so she retreated to the guest room where she had been staying since Zach's death. Her room still smelled like fresh death. She feared she would see Zach in her room if she went in there. An hour later, Granny came into the room to check on her. She brought her a plate with a tossed green salad, her favorite shrimp and pasta dish that Gary made, and her friend Betty's famous yeast rolls, which Shania loved.

She tried to get Shania to eat something, but she refused. She hadn't eaten anything since Zach's death, and now it was beginning to take a toll on her.

"You have to eat something, Shania. How do you expect to keep your strength up?" she asked her, trying to coax her into eating her favorite things. Not waiting for an answer, she continued, "I'll leave the plate here in case you change your mind," as she set the plate of food on the end table near the bed.

"By the way, some folks are asking if they could come back to see you and give their condolences since they didn't get a chance to talk to you after the service. I told them that I would check in on you to see if you were feeling up to it," Granny said, hoping she would say yes. Knowing that Shania was a family person, Granny was certain that she would feel better if she had come out of her hideout and socialized with her family and friends.

Shania shut her eyes and shook her head no as she lay in bed with her legs curled up in an almost fetal position. The comforter pulled all the way up to her neck. She was trying to hide from the world.

"It may do you some good to be around people instead of being locked up here in this room by yourself." Granny was getting worried about her.

"Granny, I can't bear people pitying me and telling me how sorry they are about Zach. I really don't feel like talking to anyone.

"Okay, baby. I'll tell them you're not up to it." Granny stopped pushing.

"I hope they understand," Shania whispered.

"They'll understand," she said as she turned to walk out the door. "Please try and eat a little something."

"I'll try," Shania replied. "I don't know what I'd do without you, Granny," Shania said, acknowledging everything Granny had done for her since childhood.

Granny was the glue that held the family together, especially during times of crisis. Although she was only five feet tall and one hundred and thirty pounds, her confidence and self-assurance made her seem bigger than life. There wasn't much that would phase her at this point.

That Tragic Day…

For the first time in a long while, Shania was in a hurry to arrive home. She hadn't felt this excited about anything pertaining to Zach in a very long time. She didn't remember the last time she had been itching to tell him something, something that she knew would make him very happy. As she pulled her car into the carport, she noticed that Zach's car was already there. Good, he's home, she thought as she hurried into the house to tell him the news that she had quit her second job.

Hello!" she called in an unusually chirpy voice. There was no answer as her voice came back to her, unheard. She walked into the kitchen, expecting to see Zach. Instead, she saw her youngest son, Zane, sitting on a stool at the counter, eating a sandwich and drinking an energy drink as he listened to music on his phone with his headphones on; that was the reason he hadn't heard his mother's greetings. She walked up behind him and pulled his headphones off his head before setting them on the counter.

"Oh, hi, Mom. I didn't see you come in," he said surprisingly.

"I know. And you didn't hear me either with that music playing so loud. Where's your dad?" Shania asked, matter of fact.

"I don't know; I guess he's not home yet," he answered, bobbing his head up and down as he picked up his headphones once again. He was too immersed in what he was listening to be bothered by anything. It was just another day, like usual.

"His car is in the port, so he must be around here somewhere. He's probably upstairs." Shania said, containing the news inside her as she searched for her husband.

"Nah, Mom, I was just up there a little while ago when I went to put my backpack in my room. He's not up there." Zane said, still occupied with his music.

"Maybe he's in the game room," she said as she opened the door to what used to be their garage. She called out to him but received no response.

"Well, he got to be home. You know that man's not going to go anywhere without his ride...Zach?" she yelled from the bottom of the stairs once again. Her voice returned back to her without any response from the other end. After two tries, she figured he must be in the bathroom. She walked over to a stool and sat down across from Zane. "Lord, I got to sit for a minute; my feet are killing me," she said as she took off her shoes and began rubbing her sore feet. After a tired day at work, searching for Zach had proved to be a tedious task. She needed a few minutes to get her strength back.

After several minutes, Shania went to the stairs and called out to Zach again. When he didn't answer, she walked over to Zane, who had his headphones back on. "Zane," she said, again pulling his headphones off, "Go upstairs, please, and see if your dad's up there. If he is, tell him that I need to talk to him." She finally gave up calling him and sought her son's help.

"Can't a man finish his meal around here...?" Zane made a face. "Dad!" he stood up and yelled before stomping up the steps.

"I tried that, remember?" Shania said exasperatedly, shaking her head at her youngest son.

A few minutes later, Zane let out a loud scream. Before Shania could make her way to the stairs, he came flying down, looking as if he'd seen a ghost. His face was pale as if the blood had been drained from his entire body.

"What in the world is going on?" she asked nervously. Her heart was pounding inside her chest as an alarm went off in her head.

"Dad…" he answered in a shaky voice as he pointed towards the steps. Zane was so traumatized by what he had seen that he couldn't even form a coherent sentence.

"What about Dad, Zane?" Shania asked hurriedly, desperately wanting to know what had happened.

I don't know. Something bad happened to him. We have to call

911," he said as he breathed in quick gasps to calm his erratic heart.

"Okay, calm down. Call 911 and tell them what you saw while I go and see what's going on." Shania coaxed her son in order to calm him down.

"No, Mom, you don't want to go up there." Zane was shaken to his core and didn't want his mother to see what he had seen.

"Just call 911, Zane; it's going to be okay," she said, already halfway up the steps.

Shania called out Zach's name as she entered their bedroom. The room was empty, so she went into the master bathroom, thinking he was in there. She figured he must have fallen while he was in there and hurt himself, which must have freaked Zane out. Nothing could have prepared her for what she saw next.

All of Zach's clothes were folded in a pile on the bathroom floor while his nude, lifeless body hung from the shower door. Shania fell back against the wall and slumped down to the floor in total shock. She put her hand over her mouth to muffle her screams. She didn't want Zane to come back up and see his father in this state again.

This can't be happening, she thought. Today was supposed to be a happy day. She had rushed home to tell Zach the good news that she had finally quit her second job. She knew he wasn't 'happy about her working two jobs and thought he would be thrilled to hear that she was going to be home to spend more time with him and their family.

She was so looking forward to being able to give more time and attention to her relationship with Zach.

"Oh my God, Zach, what have you done?" she asked as tears rolled down her face, complaining to his lifeless, cold body as if he could still hear her.

"What am I supposed to tell the kids now?" Then she remembered that Zane was downstairs calling for help. The thought horrified her to no bounds.

"Oh my God. What that poor child must be going through. Why didn't I come up here myself?" she cried. "I'd better go downstairs to see about him." She pulled herself up from the floor.

Zane stood up as Shania entered the room, still holding the phone in his hand. She rushed over to him and wrapped her arms around him, trying to protect him from what he had already been exposed to. This was her futile attempt to minimize the damage.

"Are you okay, baby?" she asked.

"I don't know, Mom. Are you?" Zane asked before he laid his head against her like he used to when he was a baby.

"I will be," she answered as she rubbed his back, comforting him."What happened up there? You don't think Dad killed himself, do you?" he asked as he looked at her with tears rolling down his cheeks. He felt so helpless, as his mind refused to believe what he saw.

"It looks that way," Shania whispered back.

"Why? Why would he kill himself? Did you find a note?" Zane asked hopefully.

"I didn't see one."

"Maybe he didn't kill himself. What if someone broke in and killed him, Mom?" Zane was still refusing to register it all.

"Let's not speculate, Zane. Let's wait until the paramedics get here. What did they say?"

"They said someone will be here shortly. I don't believe Dad would do something like that, even if he was a little weird. I'm usually the first one home. That could have been me up there." He began to cry harder, thinking about the possibility of a break-in. He was scared and ready to believe anything other than the fact that his father had taken his own life.

"Shh.., baby, we don't know what happened. Oh, God, where are they?" she said as she and Zane held on to each other while they waited for the paramedics to arrive.

After what seemed like forever, an ambulance finally pulled up with a police car in tow. The detective in charge took a brief statement from Shania and Zane, and then he and the paramedics went upstairs to check out the scene in the master bathroom.

Several minutes later, they came back downstairs and informed them there was nothing they could do and pronounced him dead. "The city coroner will be by shortly to remove the body," said the detective. "But before he gets here, I need to ask you some routine questions. What time did you arrive home?" he asked Shania.

"A little after 5:00 pm," she answered. She was shaken internally and found it hard to answer his questions.

"Was anyone here when you arrived?" he asked.

"Yes, my son was here," she said as she nodded towards Zane.

"What's your name, young man?" he asked as he turned to Zane, who was sitting next to his mom, trying to take in the news.

"Zane," he answered.

"Zane, I'm Detective Davenport. I know this is a difficult time for you, and I'm sorry for your loss. I have to ask you a few questions. Is that okay with you?"

"Yeah, I guess," Zane responded.

"What time did you get home, Zane?" he asked as he started taking notes.

"Around 3:30pm, the same time I always get home," he answered.

"Was the door locked when you arrived?"

"Yeah, we always lock our doors. My Dad makes a big deal if we forget to lock them." Zane answered.

"Who found the body?" the detective asked.

"Zane did." Shania answered, "I sent him upstairs to look for his dad; I needed to talk to him," she started crying as the whole scene played once again in her head.

"Did any of you touch anything in the bathroom?" he asked.

They both answered at the same time, "No." "And most important, did either of you find a note?" The Detective asked his final question.

Again, they both answered in chorus, "No."

After answering all of the detective's questions, Shania asked, "Do you think it was a suicide?"

"It looks that way," the detective responded, "But I can't be sure.

We'll have to wait for the coroner to make that determination."

The detective and the paramedics all left the scene except for one female officer, who remained at the house until the coroner arrived to take the body away.

"Is there anyone I can call for you?" the officer asked.

"No, I'm trying to come to grips with this before I break the news to my family," she answered, visibly shaken and distraught.

"Can I call Granny?" Zane asked. Shania nodded in approval.

After speaking with his great-grandmother, Zane handed the phone to Shania. "Mom, she wants to talk to you?"

Shania sighed as she took the phone from her son. "Yes, Granny. We're holding up the best we can... It looks like it was a suicide... No, we didn't find a note... They can't be sure; we have to wait until the coroner gets here...Okay, we'll see you when you get here. And Granny, please don't tell anyone yet. I got to get my bearings first." Shania put down the receiver as the call disconnected.

About an hour later, the coroner arrived to officially declare Zachary Andrew Taylor, Jr.'s death a suicide. The neighbors began to gather on their front porches when they saw the coroner's van parked in front of Shania's house. Granny and her son Gary pulled up just as they were loading Zach's body into the van. Shania hurried them inside before any of their neighbors could make their way over to them; she didn't want anyone to see her in this state.

Once inside, Granny pulled her into her arms and rocked her back and forth as they both cried. The telephone began to ring immediately. They just let it ring.

"I am so sorry for your loss, baby. Lord knows this family's been through enough." Granny said as she gently patted her back.

"Thank you, Granny. I'm trying to stay strong for my kids," she cried uncontrollably.

"You also must take time to grieve properly. God will take care of the kids." Granny replied. "Where's that baby? It likely gave me a heart attack when he called and told me the news." Granny inquired about Zane.

"He's in the bathroom down the hall. He's afraid to go upstairs after discovering Zach." Shania said in a raspy voice, trembling intensely.

"Oh, he's going to be afraid for a while, especially since he's the one who found him," Granny replied; she was worried about Zane, too.

"Yeah, it's gonna take some time, but he'll be all right," Gary added, trying to lighten the mood. "I remember how you were after your mama died. You were afraid of your own shadow," Gary reminded her.

"Sure was," Granny said as she spotted Zane coming into the family room. "There's my baby; come here and give Granny a big hug." She tried to cheer him up a little.

"When you gonna stop calling that boy 'baby,' Mama? He's taller than you," Gary laughed as he joined in on their hug.

"No matter how tall he is, he's still my baby. Shucks, you are taller than me, and I still call you baby, and I don't hear you complaining none," she said as she winked at Zane, fake scolding Gary.

Granny sat on the sofa as she held Shania in her arms for a while. Then she turned to her and said in a soft but serious voice, "You know, Shania, we gonna have to notify the family soon, especially Zach's mama." Granny told her matter-of-factly.

"I know, Granny."

"And we got to find a way to break it to the other kids and make arrangements for them to come home. I think it would be best if someone in the family went to pick them up. Don't you think so, Gary?"

"Mama, I think it's up to whatever Shania decides," Gary replied as he paced back and forth in front of the window, occasionally looking out at the neighbors as they gathered on their porches, curious about what they had seen.

"I haven't decided if I am going to tell them yet, Granny," Shania replied.

"You got to tell them, Shania. He's their daddy, and the sooner, the better. You don't want the family calling to tell them before you do, right?" Granny asked, trying to talk some sense into her.

"I asked you not to tell anyone yet, Granny," Shania replied, alarmed.

"And I didn't. I know it's a hard thing to accept, but you got to notify folks soon, Shania."

"I can't deal with this right now," Shania said as she rubbed her hand over her head nervously before she broke out into a cry. "I haven't had time to digest this yet. I got to go and lie down. I'll be in the guest room." She didn't have the heart to go to her room yet. She could still see him hanging there on the shower door.

"It's all right, baby; you're still in shock. You go on and lie down. We're not going anywhere." Granny said gently.

"Okay," Shania said as she walked towards the guest room. "Granny, I don't know how you made it through all your loss. I don't think I have the strength to pull through this." She said, breaking down once again.

"It was the Lord who gave me the strength to get through, and he'll do the same for you if you ask him. Go on and lie down, baby; we'll take care of things when you're feeling up to it."

"All right," Shania moaned.

Shania lay across the bed and tried to make sense of what had just happened. She kept seeing Zach's nude body hanging from the shower door. The image was so graphic and alive in her memory that she couldn't keep her eyes closed for too long. Over the years, Zach talked a lot about death, but she never suspected that he would take his own life. Nobody suspected anything like that. When his father killed himself, Zach was devastated; it was also one reason why she never thought he would put his kids through the same pain as his father did. She couldn't help but think that if she had only insisted he get help, maybe this could've been prevented.

She knew Zach was an unhappy soul long before they got married. Shania thought that her love for him would be enough. Even while they were married, Zach had dark periods when he would be consumed with depression, but at other times, he was full of life and a lot of fun to be around. This last year, he had been more depressed than she'd ever seen him. These last few months, he seemed to have sunk into a place he was unable to come back from. It was as if all joy had left him, and he had just shut the door on life altogether. Shania pleaded with him to get help. She even suggested that they go to counseling together, but he refused. She could feel him slipping away, and there wasn't anything she could do about it. Now that she was thinking about it, everything made her regret her decisions. There were so many 'what ifs' and 'if onlys' that were now haunting her.

At times, living with Zach was like living with her mother all over again. When she was eight years old, her father left, and her mother emotionally bailed out on her and her sister, Cassandra. Her mother went from being vibrant and full of life to being sad and sickly all the time. Depression was something she had seen her mother struggle through after she became ill. Shania remembered asking Granny why their mother barely talked to her and Cassy anymore. Granny told her that her mother was grieving. She didn't understand what that meant, however, and shortly after, her mama died. She never told them that she had been diagnosed with breast cancer several months before. Shania wished she could have done something to save her mother, just as she wished she could have done something to save Zach. The trauma of losing her mother had come crashing down on her all over again.

Zach was a quiet man by nature. He was tall and handsome. He was 6 feet 5 inches and weighed about 280 pounds. He was biracial with sandy-colored hair and eyes that often changed from light brown to hazel. His sturdy frame gave the impression he was a take-no-

nonsense man when, in fact, he was the opposite. Generally, he was kind and docile, never making any waves, but except on the rare occasions when he felt strongly about something, he became very determined, and nothing could change his mind.

Lately, his dark side had been showing more often with short intervals. Shania first noticed it shortly after he returned home from an early discharge from the military. He would retreat into himself and sit for hours at a time, staring into space at nothing in particular, as if he were in a trance. Then he would snap out of it as if nothing had happened. His odd behavior would stop as suddenly as it appeared. His children thought it weird, but no one had ever seen him capable of doing what he did.

Shania sat up on the bed and shook her head in an attempt to clear out the old memories. "I guess I better make that call," she said to herself as she left the guest room to call Zach's mother and her other two children.

She dreaded having to call Zach's mother to give her the news about her son, especially under the circumstances. What she dreaded the most was breaking the news to her oldest son, Trey, and her daughter, Zaria, that their dad was dead. It was going to take every ounce of strength she had, but she knew that she had to tell them. She was grateful that Granny and Uncle Gary were there. She couldn't have done it without either of them.

After the Funeral…

In the weeks following the funeral, Granny stopped by every day to check on the family and to make sure that they had enough food to eat. She was concerned about Shania and her being locked away in the guest room. She knew that she needed time to heal, and she wanted to make the healing process as easy as possible for the entire family, so she kept her thoughts to herself and refrained from making any well-meaning comments. She knew that sometimes her suggestions unwillingly came off as criticism. She realized that people just needed time and space to heal from their wounds.

The morning that Trey was leaving to return to college, Gary dropped Granny off at Shania's house so they could say their goodbyes. Granny and Zaria also made plans to spend the rest of the morning sending out thank-you cards to everyone who attended Zach's funeral. Granny knew Zaria was having a hard time coping with her father's death, and she wanted to spend quality with her, especially since Shania was finding it difficult to even take care of herself.

Granny and Zaria went into the kitchen to get started on the cards." Lord, I don't know how you all sit on these stools every day," she moaned as she climbed up on a stool.

"We can go to the dining room if you want, Granny," Zaria replied politely.

"No, I'm up here now," she answered as she pulled the sign-in book and a stack of thank-you cards out of her bag and set them on the counter. "You start with the people who signed the condolence books, and I'll take care of the ones who helped me with the repast and brought food to the house. I want to send them a special thank-you note," Granny instructed.

"Some of them probably signed one of the condolence books, too."

"Oh, I see; you're sharp, girl. You sure ain't sleeping on me none. I went over the names earlier and put a check in pencil next to the ones that I'm going to do," Granny said. She couldn't help but notice how much Zaria looked more and more like Zach as time passed. She always favored him more than the boys, but for some reason, Granny noticed the resemblance more that day, and it was uncanny.

Although Zach and Shania's three kids looked like one or the other in their own way, they all looked different; sometimes, it was hard to believe they were siblings. Their eldest son Trey had Zach's stock build, but he was on the shorter side, like Shania. He had Shania's honey-colored complexion with both Zach's and Shania's features. Zane, the youngest, was the tallest out of the three siblings. He, too, had Shania's complexion and looked like her the most. Zaria, on the other hand, was Zach's spitting image. She had his fair complexion, his sandy-colored hair, and his hazel eyes. She was also tall and on the thicker side.

"Granny, I'm really worried about Mama," Zaria said worriedly after completing a few cards.

"Oh, baby, your Mama's gonna be all right. She's just grieving. Give her some time. She'll come around." Granny coaxed.

"That's what Trey said. But I don't know. She stays in that bed in the guest room all day long. She only gets up to use the bathroom. She won't eat anything. She won't bathe, comb her hair, or anything. She looks and smells terrible, Granny. I offered to give her a bath and wash her hair, but she refused. That smell hits you as soon as you walk into that room; it's awful. And you should see how much weight she's lost. I'm afraid to leave her like this. I was thinking that maybe I shouldn't go back to school this semester." Zaria expressed her fears in detail.

This just confirmed the concern that Granny was already feeling. Hearing this, she slammed her pen on the counter and jumped off the stool. "That's it. Come, Zaria," she said.

"Where're we going?" Zaria asked, startled. "We're not done yet, are we?"

"I want you to go and run your mother a nice hot bath. Put some of that lavender that I gave you last Christmas, if you still have some, in the water. It has a calming effect on the body. She's been on that mountain long enough. It's time for her to get moving." She directed.

Granny opened the door to the guest room without knocking. The stench met her at the door. She shook her head as she headed straight for the windows.

"Go away. I said I don't need anything," Shania said from under the covers.

"Oh yes, you do. What you need is a good hot bath," Granny answered as she opened the blinds and pushed the windows up as high as they would go, trying to get rid of the godawful smell.

"What?" she said as she poked her head out from under the covers; she scrunched her eyes from the bright sun. "Granny, I thought you were one of the kids. Why are you letting all this light in here?" she asked as she ducked back under the covers.

Granny was startled by the dark circles under Shania's eyes and by how thin and narrow her face had become in just a few weeks. She tried hard not to let her surprise show. "Because you need some light and fresh air in this room. It smells worse than a pig's pen in here," she said. "Good Lord, Shania, when was the last time you bathed?"

"I took a shower last week."

"Last week? Come on; get up," she said as she pulled her covers off. Shania held on to them with the little strength she had, but she was no match for Granny, especially after the days she had spent without eating.

Granny gasped as she saw how thin she'd become. Although Zaria mentioned that her mother had lost weight, she was not prepared to see her looking like this. Shania was never a large woman, to begin with, but she had curves in all the right places. Her face was naturally full and round like Granny's, but now it was slim and scrawny.

"Oh my God, you're starving yourself to death in here. Those kids just finished burying one parent. You're trying to make it two?" Granny objected.

"Very funny, Granny."

"Oh baby, I'm not trying to be funny in the least," she said softly with tears in her eyes as she took her granddaughter into her arms. "I know you're hurting, but you got to take care of yourself, for your sake, as well as those children's. You didn't deserve any of this, and neither do they. You've got to find a way to pull it together, Shania." She held on to her and let her cry it out. Zaria came to the bedroom door several minutes later and told them that the bath was ready.

Granny nodded her head. "Zaria ran you a nice hot bath. Let's get you in it." She leaned to Shania and whispered in her ear, "She is trying to be strong for you. Let her." Then she helped her off the bed and into the bathroom. She removed her filthy nightgown and helped her into the tub. Just as Shania slumped down into the hot bath, Zaria walked in with some shampoo and conditioner for her hair.

"Zaria, you stay and help your mama get cleaned up. I'm going to go change the linens and clean up that bedroom. It smells like something died in there. Lord have mercy," she said, shaking her head as she left the bathroom. Shania and Zaria both laughed.

Night after night, Shania kept having the same haunting dream. She dreamt that Zach had found her dead. She could feel his presence standing over her and staring down at her even though she was dead. She tried to talk to him to let him know that everything was going to be all right, but no words would come out. She could feel herself trying to talk, and when she tried to open her eyes, she couldn't. Once she was able to open her eyes, she could not fall back to sleep.

She told Granny about her dream. "Granny, I can't sleep, and I'm afraid all the time. I kept having the same dream every night that Zach found me dead. I can feel myself waking up, and when I try to open my eyes, I can't."

That's what we old folks call 'the witch is riding your back.'

"I heard that before; what does that mean, Granny?" Shania asked.

"Old folks used to believe that when you can't open your eyes when you're trying to wake up, the devil has put a spell on you. But what it really means is that fear or guilt has got a hold on you, so much so that you can't sleep, and when you do fall asleep, you usually have a haunting dream immediately after falling asleep."

"But I don't have anything to feel guilty about, Granny; it's not my fault that Zach took his own life." She was confused.

"Oh, I don't doubt that for a minute, baby. But I'm not so sure that you believe that. Whatever it is that's haunting you, you got to conquer it head-on to move on." Granny advised.

"How do I do that?"

"One way is by going back to the bed that you and Zach shared. Hiding out in your guest room is doing nothing but prolonging your grief. Go ahead and grieve one time so you can move on with your life. Zach is not coming back, and it's time you face that."

Several days later, Shania sat at her kitchen counter, going over their monthly bills. She was debating whether she should contact the

27

insurance company since she hadn't heard from them since Zach's service when her phone rang. It was the funeral home calling to let her know that the insurance company had denied her claim because Zach's death was ruled a suicide. They told her she would have to pay for the services and all other expenses out of her own pocket.

Shania immediately knew that something was wrong. She distinctly remembered him saying that he wanted a no-fault policy, which meant she could collect on the policy no matter the circumstances of his death. Even though she thought it was odd at the time, she knew the no-fault policy was the reason he selected this particular company. Now she knew why.

She tried unsuccessfully to reach her insurance agent for the next several days, but he was never available to take her calls. She became anxious because the funeral home was calling her every day, asking her to make payment arrangements. She knew there was no way her family could survive without the money from Zach's insurance. When she finally did get through to them, the agent told her the company's rules changed, so they couldn't honor Zach's policy. She became frantic and called Granny for advice.

"Granny, would you believe the insurance company said they're not going to honor the claim I made on Zach's policy because he committed suicide? Zach searched around until he found a company that had a no-fault clause. Now they're saying they changed their policy." She told her frantically over the phone.

"They can't change the rules in the middle of the game. An insurance policy is a legal contract. We're not gonna take this lying down. We're going to get a lawyer to deal with them. Betty's son Noel is an estate lawyer. He handles all my affairs. He'll know what to want to do." Granny always had a solution.

"Can you please call him for me? The funeral home is calling me every day, asking for their money."

"Sure, baby, I'll call him as soon we're done. You know these things can sometimes take a while. In the meantime, you may want to consider giving the funeral home a little something until this is all cleared up. If you need anything, let me know."

"Thank you, Granny; we'll manage. I'm thinking about going back to work soon."

"I think that's a good idea. I'll give Noel a call and ask him to call you right away."

Granny was a petite woman, about 5 feet tall, and had a complexion that resembled the color of golden honey. She sported a short silver hairstyle that complemented her well. At the age of eighty-four, she had more energy than a lot of women half her age. She had lots of wisdom and was always ready to offer her advice to anyone, whether they asked for it or not.

Betty Fulton was Granny's long-time friend. They met over 25 years ago at Ebenezer Baptist Church, which they both attended. The two didn't hit it off at first. Betty thought Granny was too pushy, and Granny thought Betty was too needy.

They used to eye each other from across the church. Then, on one Easter, they were paired together and put in charge of the food preparation for the Annual Easter Pageant. They worked well together that day and have worked on various events and activities for the church ever since. Granny, who was several years older than Betty, treated her like the younger sister she never had. They became inseparable. They went on shopping sprees together, to free concerts in the park, and to the theater occasionally when Betty's son was able to get free tickets for them.

Noel Fulton was very fond and grateful for Granny. Years earlier, he had started working for a small law firm in Atlanta. Atlanta had no shortages of African American, up-and-coming lawyers, so he felt he needed to work twice as hard to be the best lawyer in the city, which gave him little time to dedicate to his parents. He was their only child. Betty Fulton was always a needy person, and she often accused Noel of being ungrateful, especially when he decided to move out and get a house of his own. When her husband was promoted to Senior Deacon, she became angry instead of being happy for him and said the church was taking up too much of his time.

Noel was glad his parents had their church family, and he was especially grateful that his mother had Granny to rely on. Betty was in relatively good shape, but Noel had to encourage her to get involved in activities constantly. She used to call on Noel, day and night, for everything. When Granny saw this, she stepped right in and told Betty that her son had an important job and that he couldn't drop his entire caseload every time she called.

Granny tried to help Betty get her focus off Noel by keeping her involved in different projects. Granny often said about Betty, "Once a woman, twice a child." When she herself had to return to her daddy's house after her first husband died, she said that was the closest she would ever get to being twice a child.

Granny couldn't have been prouder of Noel if he was her own son. Granny would send them Noel's way whenever anyone mentioned anything about needing a lawyer. When she told him about Shania's situation, he was more than happy to assist. After being unable to reach Freeland Insurance Company by phone, Noel sent them a letter confronting them about their unethical business practices. He informed them that he was going to file a lawsuit against them on behalf of Zachary Taylor's family for breach of contract. Shortly after, they sent Shania a settlement letter stating that they had paid the funeral home and to expect a settlement check in the mail within the next 7 to 10 days. Shania was so relieved. She called Noel in an attempt to pay him for his services. He refused to accept any money from her. He said that she could repay him by letting him take her out to dinner. She explained that she had just lost the love of her life, and she couldn't see herself going to dinner anytime soon. He let her know that he understood and was there for her when and if she needed a friend.

Chapter Two

Granny

Juanita Anne Johnson was born in Athens, Georgia, in the spring of 1924 to James and Bernice Johnson. She was the fifth of six children and the only girl. Most of the negroes in rural Athens at that time lived in West Hancock in framed cottage houses with only one or two rooms. They usually owned a small piece of land which they farmed. The more prosperous or middle-class negroes lived on Washington & Hull Streets, known as "Hot Corner."

Juanita's family lived in West Hancock in a three-room cottage that her father, James, built. Her father worked at one of the city's three paper mills. He eventually added running water and indoor plumbing to their cottage.

Juanita's father believed in hard work and insisted that all of his children receive a good education. He wanted more for his kids than for them to just get by. Although free education in the public school system was available, he knew that negroes did not stand a chance of receiving the same quality education that white folks received. It was a known fact that the education offered in the free black schools was inferior to the white schools in every way. The desire for equality was strong among negroes all over the country, as it was in Athens. Juanita's father was determined that his family was going to have the proper education that he didn't have. He also knew that a decent education cost money, so he worked extra hard so he could send all of them to the only private school for negroes in town. All his kids attended the private school when it was their time to go. They worked with their father in the mills every day after school. That way, the older siblings were able to help provide for their younger siblings when it was their time to attend school.

As the only girl, it was Juanita's job to help her mother with all the household chores, including taking care of her baby brother, Richie. Her mother and the younger boys did most of the farming on the weekends, while the older boys made extra money by selling whatever produce was in season to the local markets.

Working in the mills was very hard work, and at times, it could even be dangerous. There was a time when the mills wouldn't even hire negroes, so most of them, including Juanita's father, James, had to take whatever odd job they could find. It wasn't until the whites began leaving for other jobs that the mills began hiring them. When they did hire them, they were paid half of what the whites were paid. This was partly because many of them could neither read nor write. Nevertheless, they were happy to have a steady income.

Juanita's mother learned how to prepare for difficult times at an early age. Every fall, she would can whatever fruits, vegetables, and beans were in season to prepare for the winter months. She also was an excellent fisher and could out-fish most of the men in those parts. Between her mother's fishing skills and her father's hunting skills, their family did better than most negroes did for the times.

Juanita had big dreams of leaving rural Athens, Georgia, and settling in a large city. All she could think about was leaving Athens, even if it meant just going as far as Atlanta; all she wanted was to get out of her town. It was her dream to become a schoolteacher. On Sundays, she taught a Bible class at her church to the young kids for a few dollars a week. Every chance she got, she would tell the younger kids how important it was for them to have a dream and a purpose, no matter how great or small their dream was; she expressed to them that to dream was to make possibilities happen in their lives.

At the age of fifteen, she began dating a young man named Bill Evans. Bill was a friend of her eldest brother, James Junior. Bill worked at one of the mills in the town and was several years older than Juanita. He had big dreams of his own, unlike other people in Athens, and that was what had attracted her the most. He loved creating things with his hands, and he wanted to own a store where he could sell the trinkets he made from wooden scrapes. He hated working at the mills and dreamt of leaving Athens for a larger city that offered more opportunities.

Bill would stop by many evenings after supper, and he and Juanita would sit on the porch for hours and talk about their dreams. He sometimes brought her a trinket that he made from wood. Her older brothers began to leave home to either attend college or start families of their own. Her father was getting older and was unable to do all the things he used to do. Juanita's parents wanted her to quit school and take on domestic work with her mother to help out. But she loved school, and she was determined to complete her education; it was her golden ticket to becoming a schoolteacher. She would wake up at dawn and complete all her chores. Then, she would head off to school. After school, she would rush home to help her mother with the laundry that she took in for some of the wealthy white families in town. She also had to fill in for her mother at times when her mother went to take care of her sick sister, Ruth Anne, in Augusta. Juanita was a good student and a hard worker. Most days, she would breeze through her school assignments so that she and Bill could talk about their dreams if she wasn't too tired.

Being the only girl with five brothers, Juanita learned to be tough. Her father and her brothers taught her how to defend herself and stand up for what she believed in. Learning how to survive during the hard times was a skill that she learned from her mother.

Juanita graduated school at seventeen, and as soon as she turned eighteen, she and Bill got married, against her parents' wishes. They were hoping that she would stay and help them around the house, but they left Athens for Atlanta the first chance they got. By that time, all her brothers had either received their degrees and were married or were away at college working towards their degrees. She and her younger brother, Richie, were the only ones living at home.

After searching for a job, Bill ended up working in the paper mills. He hated working in the mills, but it was the only job he could get in Atlanta. While there were many other higher-paying jobs for skilled and educated blacks in Atlanta, Bill had to quit school to help support his family, like a lot of black men in rural Georgia at the time. So, he had no choice but to work in the mills once again to support himself and Juanita.

When they first arrived in Atlanta, Bill and Juanita had the time of their lives. On Saturday evenings, Bill would take Juanita to the local juke joints in town, where she had her first taste of hard liquor, which she wasn't too fond of. Up until then, she had only tasted wine around Christmas, which her father made for the occasion. What she loved about the juke joints were the dancing and the live music. Her favorite was when famous musicians like Muddy Waters or Howling Wolf came to town. She thought she had died and gone to heaven when she got to see Etta James one night after she came to town. Juanita would put on her Sunday best whenever she and Bill went into town. Most times, she was the prettiest girl in the place, and the guys were tripping over their feet to try and dance with her. But she always turned them down politely. Unfortunately, she had seen many fights that some of the men had over a pretty woman. As far as she was concerned, she was a married woman and was there to listen to the music and not to inflate any man's ego.

It wasn't long before the good times at the juke joints came to an end. Juanita became pregnant. However, she didn't see why she couldn't continue to go out dancing. She knew that she wouldn't be able to drink, which wasn't a problem for her since she didn't like the stuff anyway. But Bill wasn't having it. He said it wasn't ladylike for a pregnant woman to go to these places, music or not. Instead, he took her to the picture shows on Sunday afternoons. They would spend the entire afternoon watching westerns on the big screen, which she enjoyed. Oh, how Juanita missed those times.

Juanita became pregnant with her first child in the late 1940s. This was when women were not allowed to work while pregnant. She was working as a waitress at the five-and-dime food counter. She was able to hide her pregnancy until she was due to give birth. Juanita gave birth to a baby girl, who she named Ruth Anne, after her mother's sister. Eighteen months later, she gave birth to a second daughter, Sandra, named after Bill's mother. This time, she couldn't hide her pregnancy as well and had to leave her job as soon as her belly began to show. They decided that she would stay home to take care of the girls while Bill worked.

The pressure of working and taking care of a wife and two babies began to take its toll on Bill, so he began drinking after work with the guys from the paper mill. At first, he only drank with them on Friday evenings. Then, he started drinking every weekend. It wasn't long before he started coming home late in the evenings of the week, drunk. Knowing that Bill was under a lot of pressure, Juanita didn't confront him at first, even though she couldn't understand his frustration since her father always worked hard to support his family, and Bill wasn't doing anything out of the ordinary, according to her. She was beginning to see that Bill wasn't as motivated as he confessed to be in the early times. It didn't take long for her to realize that he was all talk.

When his drinking began to get out of hand, she felt she had no choice but to confront him. When she approached him about his drinking, he became so angry that he slapped her across her face and told her never to say a word about his activities as long as he was bringing home the bacon.

The next evening, when Bill arrived home, he noticed that the house was quieter than usual. When he inquired about the girls, she told him she put them to bed early. He smelled a familiar aroma in the air and asked what they were having for supper. She told him she had something special for him and to go and wash up while she brought his supper to the table. When he got to the table, there was a freshly baked loaf of bread and a platter piled high with fried bacon. Next to the bacon was a jar of mayonnaise and a tall glass of water.

Bill stared at the table with disbelief. He looked at her and said, "Woman, what is this? Is this some kind of joke?"

She answered in a low, husky voice, "This here is all the bacon you brought home. Let me get a knife to slice the bread with." She came back with the largest knife she could find, and in one quick motion, she plunged the knife into the loaf so hard that it broke the plate in half before pulling it out. Then she narrowed her eyes, and with the knife in her hand, she said, "If you ever think about laying a finger on me again, I'll cut your heart clear out of your chest. You enjoy your supper now," she said as she slid the glass of water across the table toward him. Bill never raised a hand to strike her again, nor did he touch a piece of bacon from that day on.

Bill continued to drink, but he limited his drinking to the weekends. He also made it a point to stay out of Juanita's way when he was inebriated.

A few years later, there was an accident down at the mill. A young man who Bill had been mentoring was working with a new power saw when his shirt got caught in it. Bill rushed over and tried to yank his shirt out when his hand slipped under the power saw, and it took his hand clean off. The men at the mill turned off the power and tied his shirt around his hand to help stop the bleeding. They rushed him way across town to the negro hospital since they knew that the hospital a few blocks away wouldn't admit negroes. What was left of his arm turned to gangrene, and they had to amputate it. A few days later, Bill succumbed to his injuries.

Juanita and her girls had to move back to Athens with her parents. Her father was not happy at her returning home with two small children, and she wasn't happy to be there either. She hated the small town even more than she had before she left.

A few months later, she left her girls with her brother James and his wife, Susie, in Hot Corner while she returned to Atlanta to find work. Negro newspapers were popping up all over the country at the time. It was a heroic and dangerous time for black journalists, even in Atlanta. Many of these newspapers were successful because negroes were interested in stories about negroes reported by negroes. They enjoyed reading about their accomplishments as much as they needed to read about who had been lynched. Juanita was able to get a job as a typist with a black-owned newspaper called The Atlanta Tribune.

Some of the men who worked there as typesetters, reporters, and journalists showed an interest in Juanita; however, she was not interested in dating anyone at the time.

Negro newspapers were popping up all over the country at the same time. Her focus was mainly on saving enough money to send for her girls. She also began taking college courses, which left her little time for courting. Unlike many other single women whose main purpose was to find a husband, Juanita was all about doing a good job in hopes of making more money.

Jackson Atkins, a prominent black businessman who was well-known around town, was the owner and senior editor for the Tribune. Jackson was born, raised, and educated in Atlanta. He attended Morehouse College, one of the most prominent negro colleges for young men. Jack, as they called him, was taken by Juanita's natural beauty, her witty personality, and her strength. Juanita was petite with a statuesque figure and hair that flowed down her back. Her golden honey skin was flawless, and her slanted eyes and beautiful smile lit up any room she walked into. Jackson noticed all the fellows at the paper, single and married, bent over backward to get her attention. They would bring her coffee, buy her lunch, and sometimes flowers to win her over. Although she accepted these items of affection gracefully, she declined their offer to take her out. She didn't want to lose sight of her goal, which was to take care of her girls. When she told them of her plans to send for her girls when she was financially able, they began to shy away. Some of them were even intimidated by her strong will, but Jackson found this attractive.

Jackson's first wife and child died during childbirth. He remained single and kept himself busy by working hard to help improve the lives of his fellow brothers. He was tall, dark, and handsome, with dimples that you could see a mile away. He never had any trouble attracting women. After losing what he considered to be the perfect wife, he thought he would never meet anyone who could measure up to her. He felt that women were only interested in him because of his position. His mother's overbearing nature and his fear of becoming like his father also contributed to his feelings of insecurity.

The more that Jackson worked with Juanita, the more he became smitten with her. Although she was smart, witty, and beautiful, the thing that attracted him the most was that she was all about the business.

With her girls living in Athens, she was able to work longer hours and often worked late in the evenings when she didn't have class. Jackson took this time to get to know her better. When she did work late, she would bring in food for her supper, which she generously shared with him. He eventually asked her out for a date. At first, she was reluctant because she didn't want anyone to think she was trying to get in good with the boss. However, Jack kept asking her out until, finally, his determination wore her down, and she accepted his invitation.

Jackson and Juanita had been dating for several months when he hinted to his mother that he was thinking about asking Juanita for her hand in marriage. His mother had reservations about Juanita, and she let it be known that she didn't trust her. This wasn't unusual since his mother found fault in anyone who showed an interest in her son. His mother was a strong woman, much like Juanita, who worked hard to raise and educate him and his two sisters after their father drank himself to death. His mother saw herself competing with Juanita for her son's attention.

One evening, when he and Juanita talked about her bringing her kids to Atlanta and the possibility of marriage, he told her that his mother had previously scared most of his dates away and didn't approve of anyone he dated except for his first wife. She told him that she could understand that since Jackson still lived under her roof, even if it was in her basement. Juanita suggested that it may be time for him to cut the apron strings and get a place of his own. But he told her that his mother was getting older and needed him, so he was going to remain in his mother's basement. Shortly after that, he asked her to marry him. She declined, telling him that she needed a man and her girls needed a father, not a puppy being led around on a leash.

Six months later, Jackson bought a three-bedroom ranch house on the other side of town from his mother; then, he asked her to marry him again. This time, she accepted.

Juanita had a small but beautiful wedding, which she didn't have with her first husband. They were married at her newfound Ebenezer Baptist Church. Her parents were older, and they were unable to attend her wedding because of their health issues. Her brother James walked her down the aisle. He and Susie brought her girls, who ended up staying in Atlanta with them.

Juanita continued to work at the Tribune until she became pregnant with her and Jack's first child together. They had a son whom they named Jackson Jr. They called him JJ for obvious reasons. Two years later, she gave birth to their second son, Gary. Her daughters were ten and eight by this time.

The Tribune was becoming very popular. Folks were excited to read about real issues that negroes faced every day. The Atlanta Tribune began reporting on stories about the Ku Klux Klan and the lynchings that were taking place around the country. At the time, Atlanta, Georgia, was the home of the KKK headquarters. The KKK didn't like these stories and began threatening their paper. Although they continued reporting on the issues that were affecting their communities, they began to meet in private to discuss ways to warn those potentially in danger of the KKK. Whenever anyone at the Tribune received word on which city a lynching was going to take place, they would write about it in code in their paper. They used rivers, lakes, natural landmarks, or structures in the city as a clue as to where the lynching was going to take place. They listed various places where intended victims could migrate too.

As the owner and the senior editor of the Tribune, Jack decided which stories should be included in the paper. What they didn't know was that their junior editor was feeding information to the editor of the local white rival newspaper, who just happened to be the son of the leader of Atlanta's KKK Chapter.

The KKK began to hijack the Tribune's delivery trucks and grab all the newspapers before roughing up their drivers. It wasn't until after two very public high jackings that they realized they were being set up. When they figured out who their mole was, they immediately fired him.

A few weeks later, their building was bombed with Jackson and a few other staff of The Atlanta Tribune inside. The former junior editor was also killed that night when his house was bombed just a few blocks away. Juanita was a widow once again. She had lost two husbands by the age of thirty-five.

Jackson left the house to Juanita, which was completely paid for, along with a modest insurance policy, which he hoped would allow her to stay home and care for the boys until they were of school age.

When her finances started to run out, Juanita began to apply for jobs at other black newspapers, but no one would hire her for fear they would meet the same fate as Jackson. It became harder and harder for Juanita to find work. The only people who were willing to hire her were those who needed someone to do domestic work, which she refused to do. She watched her mother take in the laundry for white folks when she was younger, and she refused to do domestic work for anyone. So, she was forced to take odd jobs to support her family.

Her goal, like her father's, was for all her kids to get a decent education, even if it meant that she had to work hard for this to happen, which, for the most part, she did.

After Juanita's oldest daughter, Ruth Anne, graduated high school, she headed out west to the University of California, which had just begun accepting negroes at the time. Ruth Anne went there to pursue her teaching degree. Her second daughter Sandra attended Spelman College there in Atlanta. Jackson, Jr. had no desire to attend college, so against her wishes, he joined the Navy instead. Gary, her youngest, received his degree in business from Clark University in Atlanta.

Just when things were looking up for her, the unspeakable happened. Juanita, who was no stranger to tragedy, was hit with the worst tragedy anyone could imagine. She lost her son, Jackson, Jr., and her daughter, Sandra, within six months of each other.

Chapter Three
Zach and Shania

Zach knew he was adopted long before his mother told him. As a kid, he always felt that he was different, especially since he didn't look like anyone in his family. When he was eight years old, he went looking for his birth certificate for a class project and came across it in his parent's closet, along with his adoption papers. He asked his father about them, and his father became very angry and told him that he should be thankful that they adopted him because his real parents didn't want him. He warned him not to tell his mother. He said it would only upset her.

However, Zach couldn't keep the news about his adoption to himself, so he told one of his classmates, who told his sister. His sister thought that he was making up stories and asked her father about what she heard. Zach's father, who was often verbally abusive, became enraged and gave Zach the beating of his life. Despite all the verbal abuse, he had never raised a hand to Zach before, so this was traumatizing for him, especially since he could not turn to his mother for comfort because his father forbade him to tell her. Zach knew at this point what his father was capable of, so he dared not say a word.

After this, he felt he was all alone, with no one to turn to or trust. He soon discovered that he was the only one of his siblings who was adopted. For the first time in his life, he felt as if he didn't belong. This plagued him for the rest of his life.

Zach's parents, Ella and Zachary, Sr., had been married for several years before having children. Ella was convinced that she was unable to have any. Young men everywhere were being drafted into the Vietnam War, and she thought if they had a child and his father was the sole provider, he would be able to get out of going to war. So, she quit her teaching job, and they adopted an infant named Zachary, Jr. To their surprise, Zach, Sr., was drafted six months later.

Shortly after he left to go overseas, Zach Jr.'s mother found out that she was pregnant. They had a daughter, Rhonda. Two years later, they had a son, whom they named Theodore. Zach's father served for several years before coming home as a decorated veteran. He received several medals for bravery. His reward was mental illness.

Shania and Zach began dating in high school. Even though Zach was one of the best-looking guys in the school, he wasn't popular. He was tall and handsome. He looked as if he could have been biracial. He was not sociable and was unusually quiet for a teen. Everyone thought that he acted strangely. Shania was also quiet and shy. She felt like she lived in her older sister Cassandra's shadow. Cassandra was very popular and outgoing. She was smart and was always surrounded by lots of friends. Shania always looked up to her and felt that she could never measure up to her.

Shania and Zach met by an odd coincidence. Zach was sitting on the grass with his back against a tree in the schoolyard, reading a book while eating his lunch, when Shania walked up to him. She told him she was trying to get out of the sun and asked if he minded if she sat next to him. "Sure," he said as he moved to one side of the tree, giving her the other side to lean against.

"Why are you sitting here instead of hanging with your friends?" he asked.

"Because I want to finish reading my book. It's really good. My friends all think I'm goofy for wanting to read instead of standing around gossiping with them."

"Well, isn't that what you girls do?" he asked, intrigued.

"No, not all of us girls. What about you? I haven't met a boy yet who would rather read instead of standing around and watching all the girls with his friends."

"Why should I stand around and make it obvious that I'm watching when I can sit here and watch, and nobody knows I'm watching?"

"Eeeww, that's creepy. Is that what you do? We like it when you're watching us, and we know you're watching. Don't you know anything about girls? Aren't you a senior?"

"No, I'm a junior. By the way, my name's Zach, and I know plenty about girls."

"I'm Shania, and I'm a freshman. Well, I gotta get going. It was nice meeting you. So much for reading," she said as she smiled and ran off to tell her friends about the cute junior she had just met. Once she caught up with her friends, she pointed him out. They said that he was cute but too quiet and strange. Shania didn't find him strange at all.

She thought he was intelligent and just misunderstood. She was determined to find out all she could about him.

This was a very lonely time for Shania at home, especially since her sister Cassandra was away at college. It was just her and her grandmother. She worked part-time after school at the library and spent a lot of time reading. But she secretly craved male attention.

One afternoon, when she was at the library reading a book, Zach slipped into the chair next to her. "Reading something exciting?" he asked.

"No, I'm reading Socrates," she answered, trying to hide her excitement.

"I'm impressed. Most people don't like ancient literature. I'm a real fan of Roman and Greek Literature, myself."

"I'm not. I have to read this for my English Lit. class. I'm only halfway through, and I don't understand a thing I'm reading. What makes it so bad is that I'm having a test on it next week."

"You must have Mrs. Hamilton. She's a real maniac when it comes to this stuff. I can help you understand it if you like."

"Would you?"

After Zach helped Shania understand Socrates, they became fast friends. They talked almost every day. They met at the library on the days that she didn't have to work. In the evenings, they talked on the phone into the wee hours. He helped her with her class assignments whenever she needed it. This was the most attention Shania had ever received from a male, and she was enjoying every minute of it.

A year later, they went on their first date to the movies. At first, Granny gave her a hard time. She thought it was proper for her to meet him first. This didn't stop Shania; she was enjoying the attention.

Zach had a lot of hobbies and hidden talents. He loved jazz, and he was in a band with some college students across town. On the days Shania was at work, he often practiced with the band. He played the saxophone and the trombone. He was also a star student in mathematics and was slated for college scholarships to some of the best schools in the nation. During his junior year, he was instrumental in helping his school solve a complicated mathematical project, after which the Dean put his name in for scholarships.

Even after all of that, Zach had little confidence in his own abilities. He thought of himself as the child no one wanted. He didn't know what he wanted to do after he graduated, except that he wanted to spend the rest of his life with Shania.

Shania knew that she had to finish high school before she could think about marriage. She also knew her grandmother wouldn't hear of her getting married so young. She wanted Shania to experience life before settling down instead of getting tied down to the first boy she met the way she and Shania's mother did.

Zach was thoughtful and kind. He had a special talent for writing, and he wrote poetry for Shania every chance he got. He brought her flowers and gifts for her birthday, Christmas, and Valentine's Day. All her friends, who thought he was strange at first, began to envy their relationship.

Zach thought long and hard about what he wanted to do with his life. Since Shania wasn't ready to get married yet, he decided that he wanted to join the Army. His father was in the Army, and he wanted to do the same so that he would feel closer to him.

Shania was devastated when Zach told her of his decision to join the Army. She tried to persuade him to take the scholarship that Morehouse College offered him instead of serving in the military, but he said his mind was made up. The more she and his mother pleaded with him to stay in Atlanta and take the scholarship, the more determined he became to get away.

Morehouse College was one of the best black colleges in the country, and it was in Atlanta, Georgia. To be offered a full scholarship was a huge deal. His decision not to take it seemed very strange, to say the least.

In 1973, the draft system in the United States was abolished, making the Armed Forces an all-volunteer military. Many young people joined the military to pay for their education afterward or as a way to stay out of trouble. Neither was the case with Zach since he was never in trouble and was offered full scholarships to some of the best colleges in the country. Zach wanted to follow in his father's footsteps in hopes that it would make him a stronger man, so he volunteered to join the Army.

After Zach left for basic training, Granny tried everything she could to get Shania to date other young men, but Shania refused. She even tried to set Shania up with some of her friends' sons, but Shania's heart was set on waiting for Zach. Granny hoped and prayed that Zach felt the same way and didn't have a change of heart or meet someone else while he was away.

At first, basic training seemed good for Zach. He was pleased with the discipline the Army was trying to instill in them. Then he started to notice that some of the enlistees didn't seem to take the military very seriously. Many of them began to play jokes on each other, while others, like Zach, took the military seriously.

During the first week, while stationed at Fort Honeywell in East Texas, Zach met Ricardo Andrews, who everyone called Rico. It didn't take them long to notice the racism that ran rampant in their unit. Although he and Rico were complete opposites, they formed a bond, mainly out of necessity, which was common for blacks serving in the military.

Zach was very tall, and he had a light complexion with hazel green eyes. He had a thick build, was easy-going, and laid back. Rico, on the other hand, was short, very dark, and scrawny. He was also loud and rambunctious.

Although the military was integrated, many units were voluntarily divided by race: whites, blacks, and Hispanics. From the day they arrived, Rico was the brunt of everyone's jokes because of his very dark skin. Other blacks ridiculed him to keep the insults off themselves. The

Hispanics insulted him because they thought they were a grade better, and the whites were cruel because that's the way things still were, especially in the South. Rico, who has been ridiculed all his life because of his dark skin, expected nothing less. He always had his defenses up, ready to give as much as he took.

Zach was occasionally ridiculed by other African Americans because of his light skin. They called him a white boy and would refer to him as the white tiger because of the color of his eyes. Zach, however, never experienced anything as harsh as the bullying that Rico had to endure. His bunkmates and superiors alike called Rico every kind of derogatory name there was. He was the target of all their cruel jokes.

At first, Rico accepted the bashing and jokes good-heartedly, but when Rico began to lash out with racial jokes of his own, he and other black soldiers began finding racist notes taped to their bunks. They even received death threats.

One evening, Rico and another soldier arrived at their dorm to find a black male blow-up doll with noose tied around its neck. Rico demanded to know who put it there. When no one admitted to putting the doll in the dorm, he knew what he needed to do. He went to his Commanding Officer and demanded that he put a stop to the racism. He told them that the incident with the noose was crossing the line. When the commander downplayed the incident, Rico went on a rampage. He went back to the bunkers and overturned the cots of all the men who were not black and urinated on them. He was given 10 days in the stockade. After he was released from the stockade, he lost some of his privileges and was not allowed to leave the base for two weeks. He took this time to write to several high-ranking officials in his chain of command, asking them to investigate the extreme racism that he and others had to endure. His Captain told him that there was going to be an investigation. Just when he thought something was finally going to be done, he was killed by friendly fire.

A team of men, including Rico and Zach, was sent into the woods for survival training; somehow, they got separated, almost as if it were planned. Just when Zach noticed that Rico wasn't with them, he heard a gunshot. He took off running in the opposite direction of the shot. When he realized someone was still shooting, he dove into the nearest bush. A bullet grazed him, and pieces of the metal from the bullet had entered his right shoulder. Several minutes later, he saw two soldiers carrying Rico's body out of the woods. The story that was told was that hot-headed Rico wandered off and was shot by someone firing at what they thought was a wild animal about to attack.

Everyone knew that the woods were supposed to be cleared before any military personnel entered for training. In reality, the team was heading in one direction when suddenly they heard a command to "about-face" when Rico was several feet out of earshot. Zach didn't know why the shooting began, but he did know that there weren't any wild animals anywhere in sight.

Zach was not only devastated by Rico's death, but he had serious doubts that it was an accident. Rico had a big mouth and was not well-liked. He constantly challenged his superiors.

Zach questioned his commander about the reported friendly fire incident. His commander dismissed him with a stiff warning not to stir up trouble. This response made Zach more suspicious, and as a result, he became more and more depressed. He requested to be discharged because of his minor injuries. His request was denied. So, he took his suspicions to any and everyone who would listen. His questions made his superiors so uneasy that they eventually agreed to give him an honorable discharge and sent him packing. Zach accepted the early discharge, glad to be going home after only a year and a half with just minor injuries.

Zach began dealing with a tremendous amount of fear after he returned home. His father, a Vietnam survivor, received several medals for bravery and suffered from Post-Traumatic Stress Syndrome (PTSD), known as "shell shock." He returned home with an extreme amount of anxiety. Several months out of the year, he seemed normal, but during the hot, humid summer months, his mind flashed back to the swamps of Vietnam. He spent hours roaming the conservation parks in Atlanta. He would duck behind the trees and bushes and would suddenly jump out, yelling at the top of his lungs. The police had to be called several times. Those times were hard on the family and intolerable for him. He eventually killed himself. Zach, who was a teenager at the time, never got over his father's death. The older he became, the more he feared that he was becoming angry and shell-shocked like his father.

When Zach first went into the Army, he wrote Shania letters at least once a week. She lived for his letters and his poetry. She vowed that she was going to have them published as a gift for him one day. Then the letters suddenly stopped. After he stopped writing to her, he began calling her. He told her about losing his best friend. He was afraid and became paranoid, thinking he was going to be next. Shania was afraid for him as well and worried constantly about his well-being.

Zach finally came home. He was released on an early discharge. He had a terrible experience in the Army, but once he got back, he refused to talk about it with Shania. Instead, he became clingy, and he wanted to be around her every waking moment. At first, this did not bother Shania. She loved all the attention that she was getting from him. Granny, on the other hand, became worried about Zach's dependency on Shania. She thought about her first marriage and how she married right after high school. She knew that marrying Bill was her ticket out of Athens. She wanted more for Shania. She wanted her to spread her wings and live life a bit before settling down. What she wanted most was for her to complete college.

At first, Zach wanted Shania to move in with him, but she refused. She knew Granny wouldn't allow her to shack up with anyone, so Zach and Shania were married shortly after his return, but in a short time, Shania noticed a change in him. His behavior was very different, and sometimes, it was hard to believe that he was the same person. She gave him an edge by thinking that maybe it was because they got married too soon.

Although Shaina was aware of Zach's weird behaviors, it wasn't long after they were married that Shania became aware of Zach's nightmares. The first time she witnessed it, it scared her halfway to death.

They were both asleep in bed when suddenly, he woke up screaming at the top of his lungs. Then he stopped just as suddenly as he had begun as if nothing had happened. The funny part was that he didn't even remember the nightmare or screaming the next day. One time, he even jumped out of bed, cursing and throwing punches in the air. She had to duck to keep from getting punched.

Shania was so frightened by his strange behavior that she started recording him so he could hear it for himself. She finally insisted that he seek help if they were to stay married. So, Zach went to see a therapist and told him about all his past traumas and his friend getting killed. The Doctor explained that he was having nightmares, which were caused by post-traumatic stress disorder. He was told that this wasn't uncommon for a person who experienced a traumatizing event such as he did. He said that the terrors could eventually go away, and in time, they did, at least for a while.

Zach started to work in the registration office at Georgia State during the day and attended classes in the evenings. He went on to receive a degree in Mathematics. Then, he began working as an accountant for the state of Georgia. In just a short time, he worked his way up to the Chief Accountant. Meanwhile, Shania did not complete her studies at Spelman; she did, however, receive a real estate license. She began selling townhouses to young single persons. Shania did well in her career, but she felt like something was missing in her life. She wanted to fill the empty void in her heart with a child. She wanted a family.

Their first child, Zachary III, whom they called "Trey," was born a year later. Three years later, their second child, their daughter Zaria, was born. Two years later, they had a second son, Zane. To accommodate their growing family, they purchased a beautiful five-bedroom modern Tudor home in a quiet, upscale suburban neighborhood outside of Atlanta.

Shania was determined to create the typical upper-middle-class family. They both had successful jobs and were able to balance hard work while raising their family. During the first decade of the new millennium, the real estate market began to decline across the country, and as the housing bubble burst, many real estate companies took a hit. The company Shania worked for went out of business, and she was out of work for a few months. Fortunately, with Granny's connections, she was able to find another job.

Zach and Shania continued to work hard as they raised their family. Several years later, just as their oldest son was about to graduate from high school, Zach suddenly decided that he wanted a change in his career. He said that he was tired of working for the state. He felt that 20 years was more than enough time to give to a job. He and his long-time friend Arthur wanted to open up their own janitorial service.

With their oldest son about to go away to college, Shania was skeptical because she felt that they couldn't afford the risk. They needed two secure incomes. She was concerned that Zach was making another impulsive decision like he did when he upped and joined the Army. Zach insisted he couldn't last another year with the State. Zach, who was laid back and easygoing, usually went along with most of Shania's ideas, so against her better judgment, she decided to show her support for him, even though it meant that they had to invest money into this new business. As a precaution, Zach was able to put in for a temporary leave with the state as a way to secure his position.

Zach and Arthur met while playing in a jazz band together. The band was put together by his former church's choir teacher. He and Arty remained friends even after the band was dismantled. Arty was a tall, stocky man with a booming voice. His voice had a bass to it, and people often heard him before they saw him. Over the years, he worked various jobs as a janitor and eventually ended up working as head janitor for a large private company. He shared with Zach his interest in wanting to become an entrepreneur by opening his own cleaning service. He told him that with his experience and Zach's accounting knowledge, they could open a cleaning business of their own. His goal was to hire a cleaning crew and eventually snag a few government contracts to clean their offices. This piqued Zach's interest, and eventually, he was able to convince Shania to allow him to pursue his dream of becoming an entrepreneur.

Zach's new career venture turned out to be much more challenging than he and Arty expected. First, they had to invest more money than they originally planned for the business to take off. Once it did, Zach found that he had to do more than just secure the contracts and keep their books. Since money was tight, they were unable to hire as much cleaning staff as they needed, so Zach had to pitch in with the cleaning. This did not go well with Zach. After working on the other side of the desk for 20 years, he wasn't used to getting his hands dirty.

It also didn't take him long to discover that working with Arty wasn't so easy. Arty worked as a head janitor for several years and was used to giving orders. Zach, on the other hand, wasn't used to taking them, especially from what he considered a janitor. He complained to Shania about Arty being bossy and that he spent more time telling him what to do than he did cleaning.

Even though the first year was difficult, Zach was able to get a few contracts, which allowed them to hire more staff. They were able to stay afloat; however, they did not achieve the cash flow that Zach had hoped for.

By the third year, they were seeing a larger profit. Zach, who had a good head for business, became bored and impatient, so he decided it was a good time to sell his share of the company. He had taken a leave from the State, so he was able to return to his old job. When he returned to the state, the position he had previously held was filled with a much younger and less experienced person, so he was assigned to a different position. Zach had a hard time adjusting to his new position. He became increasingly depressed and unhappy at work. Shania tried to persuade him to see his new position as a new challenge, but he couldn't see it that way.

Although Zach sold his half of the janitorial company, it would take a few months before he received all his money. He thought it would be best for Zaria to put off going to college for at least a year. She was in her senior year of high school. He figured this would give them some time to get settled financially.

Shania was disappointed with Zach's decision to sell his half of the janitorial business, but she was not surprised, considering his track record of making rash decisions. But when he started talking about Zaria, putting off going to college for a year, Shania would not hear of it. She explained to Zach that Zaria had her heart set on going away to college. She was a straight-A student. She applied for full scholarships. Zach wasn't confident that she would get it. All he saw was another expense. Reluctantly, he agreed with Shania, but the stress that he was feeling caused him to retreat into himself.

Zaria received a full scholarship to Tuskegee University in Alabama, which was just two hours from Atlanta. This good news did nothing to ease Zach's anxiety, and he became more dissatisfied with life. It wasn't long before his nightmares returned. His PTSD got so bad that his screams routinely woke up the entire household. Shania suggested that he see a therapist again, but Zach wouldn't hear of it. Instead, he became more and more distant from the family and stopped participating in any family gatherings. He even refused to eat at the dinner table with them as a family, which was something they both always insisted on. His day consisted of going to work and coming home just to spend his time in the den on his computer.

The kids began noticing a change in his behavior. Zane, the only one left at home, complained the most. He said he was embarrassed to bring his friends to the house anymore, let alone ask them to stay

61

overnight because his father "acted weird," and he didn't want to have to explain to his friends why his father didn't act normal. Zaria complained that he was looking at "weird things" on the computer, and Trey said he had seen him in front of their house talking to himself.

Zach, who had always handled the household finances, began to neglect their bills. Shania had no choice but to take them over and make sure they weren't delinquent. When Zach didn't protest her handling their bills, she started to feel like she didn't know him anymore. After all, he was an accountant. Instead of discussing her concerns with him, Shania drove more and more into taking care of their household as well as her work so she wouldn't have to deal with his issues.

With Trey in his senior year at Clark University and Zaria in her freshmen year at Tuskegee in Alabama, Shania had to admit that their finances were getting a little tight, not to mention the loss that they sustained from Zach's business mishap. She knew that with Zach's state of mind, he was not in any position to handle the additional stress, so she decided to take on a second job, one because she knew that she had to do something about their financial situation and secondly because she couldn't deal with Zach's mental decline. Taking on a second job was her way of handling her family's problems.

Shania taught a real estate course two evenings a week and on Saturday mornings, which she really loved. Zach had always agreed to whatever she wanted, so she didn't even bother discussing her new job with him. When he found out that she was working two jobs, much to her surprise, he became furious.

One evening, when she arrived home from work, she saw a side of him she had never seen before. She walked into the kitchen and found Zach sitting on the stool with his face in his hands. She put her hand on his shoulder and asked if he was all right. He looked up at her with a look on his face that she had never seen.

"Don't touch me," he nearly growled. Shania jumped as she pulled her hand back, startled by his response.

"What's wrong, Zach? Are you feeling all right?" she asked.

"No, I am not. I'm sick and tired of your secrets and lies, Shania."

"Secrets and lies. What the hell are you talking about?" she asked, afraid of his strange behavior and yet refusing to back down.

"Where are you going on the evenings that you aren't coming straight home? And don't you dare lie to me," his eyes had the look of agony.

"I've been working a second job, Zach." She answered as she tried to stay calm.

"When were you planning to tell me this, Shania?"

"I didn't think it mattered. What's the big deal?" Shania said nervously.

"You didn't think it mattered?" he yelled. 'What's the big deal? The big deal is how it makes me look when my wife's working two jobs and I only have one. It makes me look like I can't support my family; that's how it looks." He banged the table with his fist.

63

"I just wanted to help us get rid of some of our debt. I found something that I'm good at and actually enjoy doing, so I went for it."

"And you didn't think enough of me to mention that you had a second job? Since when do we do things without discussing them with each other? Have I ever denied you anything, Shania?"

"No, you haven't, Zach."

"No, I haven't," he said as if he didn't hear her answer. "You already took over handling the bills. Did I object? You've always called the shots around here, and yet you still felt the need to keep your second job a secret from me." He looked dead straight into her eyes.

"I knew you'd been under a lot of stress lately, Zach. I just did what I thought was best for all of us."

"You always do what you think is best for us. But at least before you had the decency to tell me about it. What are you doing, saving up money to leave me?"

"Oh, come on, Zach; you know I would never do anything like that."

"Do I?"

"You're right, Zach; I should have discussed getting a second job with you, and I'm sorry. But I have been trying to get you involved in making decisions around here for years. Every time I ask you anything, all you do is tell me to do whatever I want. So, I took it for granted that you would be okay with this. I'll quit the job if you want me to." She sounded helpless.

"No, you don't have to quit your job. That's not necessary," Zach said, calming down. "You're already working. But next time, would you please let me know before you make any major decisions around here?"

"Okay, I promise, Zach," Shania said as she leaned over and kissed his cheek. "Are you hungry? Let me make you some dinner." She said as she moved towards the stove.

"That won't be necessary. I'm not hungry," he said before putting his head down on the counter.

Chapter Four
Getting Back On Track

Shania still dreamt about Zach every night, but her dreams were not as intense. She knew that what Granny told her was true; it was time for her to move forward, so she returned to her and Zach's bedroom.

Shania went back to work after taking a month off to grieve and get her family back on track. Everyone at her workplace was very supportive during her hard time. She was grateful that she had a job to go back to, especially since she had only worked there for a few years prior to Zach's death.

Shania had previously worked for a real estate company but lost her job after it folded due to their predatory lending practices. Unfortunately, her company was one of the main offenders. It had a history of selling homes and townhouses to people who lived out of state with little or no down payment required, after which the company would raise its rates, leaving homeowners unable to keep up with their mortgage. Eventually, the company was sued, and as a result, they had to file for bankruptcy and had to lay all their employees off.

Shania wasn't out of work for long, thanks to Granny's connections. One of Granny's church sisters worked for an organization that helped single mothers in need of housing and food. The company was looking to recruit employees with various skills. Granny told them about Shania's background in real estate. Shania was interviewed and was hired. Her job was to educate and teach young women how to manage and navigate their credit and, in some cases, get their credit in order so they would be able to achieve their goals.

Tricia Williams was the founder of Destination, a women's intervention program that specialized in helping women secure jobs, housing, and childcare. They also offered counseling to the women as well. She and her husband, Jake, were co-pastors of 'Our Lady of Grace'

Church in Atlanta. Shania was happy to be a part of an organization that specialized in working with single mothers to help them increase their skills so they could obtain jobs. They were taught various computer programs so they could be able to work in an office as nursing assistants or in any other field they may be interested in.

It was a modest-size company with the potential for expanding. Presently, there were 20 employees who had expertise in various skills, like housing or computer specialist, therapy, and teachers of adult literacy education.

Shania enjoyed working with these women by helping them to get and maintain financial credit so that they could be able to achieve their dream. Tricia was a wonderful person to work for. She was secure and confident, and everyone at the company loved and admired her. Regardless of the kind of day she was having, she always had a word of encouragement for her employees. Her motto was that happy employees made good workers. Her positive attitude was infectious. Most of the people who worked at Destination were willing to go the extra mile because of her example.

Several of the staff members were from the Church that she and her husband Jake co-founded. Many felt this job gave them a second chance at life. A few weeks after Shania settled back into work, Tricia invited her to lunch. Shania gladly accepted. They went to a small café named Palm's, a few blocks from the office.

"I hope it's all right that we came here," said Tricia politely. "I chose it because it's close by."

"Oh yeah, this is fine with me." Shania smiled.

"Good. You know, I'm glad we got this chance to get together, Shania. We haven't had time to really talk since you've been back," Tricia said. "How are you and your family doing?"

"We're adjusting." Shaina lowered her gaze. "Thanks for asking Tricia. I really appreciate all your support."

"It's my pleasure. We're like family here, and I just wanted you to know you're not alone," she said just as the waiter arrived to take their order. Shania ordered a Caesar salad and a sweet tea. Tricia ordered their chicken wrap with a diet coke.

"Are the kids back in school, or are they going to take the rest of the semester off?"

"They're back in school. Trey went back a few weeks ago. He was eager to get back to work. He's working part-time between his classes. Zaria went back this past weekend. I think it'll do them good to resume some normalcy. Zane is still having a hard time right now. But I guess that's to be expected."

"I'm sure it is. Have you considered sending him to counseling?" she asked reluctantly.

"I tried to get him into counseling, but he refuses to go," Shaina told her.

"Well, our Church offers counseling. We have trained professionals. You should check them out," Tricia said as she reached into her pocket for a business card.

"Don't you have to be a member of the church?" Shania asked as she took the business card from her.

"No, not at all; our Church's outreach programs are open to anyone who's interested. We also have someone you can talk to. Maybe they can help you get through your grieving process."

"I tried counseling before, and then I stopped; I'm not ready to share my pain with a stranger yet," she said in a low voice.

"I understand how difficult that can be. When I was going through my loss, God was the only one I could talk to for a long time. Then, he directed me to a church that was instrumental in helping me get back on track. I give God praise every day for placing that non-denominational Church in my life." Tricia replied.

"What are the beliefs of the non-denominational church?" Shania asked.

"Well, for one, they accept all people who believe in Christ. Whether they be Catholic, Baptist or Protestant."

"Is that what your church is, a non-denominational church?" Shaina asked curiously.

"Actually, the Church Jake and I co-founded is an Interfaith Church, which welcomes people of all faiths, not just Christians. In the Bible, there was no such thing as Catholics, Baptists, or Muslims; as long they were believers in God, followed his commandments, and did not worship false idols, they had his blessing.

Shania, everyone goes through some kind of struggle in life. Life can be hard, but when we believe in something higher than ourselves, it helps make things easier for us. Some people's struggles are worse than others, but this is God's way of helping us to develop character," Tricia explained.

"What I don't understand is if God is supposed to be this all-loving God, then why does he cause people to suffer?" Shania asked as she looked blankly at her.

"God doesn't cause people to suffer. He allows us to make choices. Each and every one of us is born with free will. We have the will to make choices in our lives, good or bad. Our choices determine our outcomes. Then there are times when we will suffer because of another person's bad choice." Tricia said as she held Shania's hands gently.

"Don't I know it?" Shania said.

"And there are times when God steps in and changes the situation completely around. I'm sure you've heard or know of someone who had been diagnosed with a terminal disease, and then suddenly, their situation completely changed until there was no sign of the illness." Her grip on her hands got a little affirmative.

"Yes, I have, but why does he do that for some people and not others?" Shania asked, puzzled.

"It has to do with our level of faith. God wants us to trust him and believe all things work together for the good, even when we don't have all the answers," she said as the waitress arrived with their food. She took a few minutes to say grace for them both before continuing.

"When Jake and I lost Jacob, he was only two years old. It was New Year's Eve of 1984 Jake's sister Jackie's birthday. She turned 25 and decided to throw herself a New 's Eve party. As a rule, Jake and I didn't drive anywhere on certain holidays because of drunk drivers, but he insisted on showing his support for his baby sister. His mother was in town, and she wanted to bring the New Year in with all her grands So, his mother and Jackie fixed up a bedroom at the house for all the kids to stay in while the adults partied.

I was just getting over the flu and wasn't feeling up to attending, so I told him that I would stay home with the baby. Besides, I didn't want to take a two-year-old to a New Year's Eve party. But Jake insisted on taking him. He said his mother was looking forward to seeing all her grandchildren, and he didn't want to disappoint her. I told him that I wasn't comfortable with him taking Jacob because I was afraid that something might happen to him. I don't know why, but I just had this nagging feeling. He thought I was overreacting and assured me they would be okay since his sister lived only 15 minutes away.

Well, the Devil's always busy. He heard the fear in my voice that night and used it against me. They weren't even gone but 10 minutes when a drunk driver ran a light and plunged into the car. This was when frontal were relatively new. Jacob was in his booster seat in the front next to Jake. The airbag was at the same level as Jacob's face. It exploded, and when it inflated, it made contact with his face. The gas from the bag caused third-degree burns to his face and chest. The material used for airbags at that time was deemed unsafe. He lived for eight days before an infection set in, and he died," she said as she wiped tears from her cheeks. "The following year, the first child passenger safety law was passed.

Jake wasn't hurt nearly as badly. Both his arms were broken, and he suffered contusions to his chest. But he took Jacob's death the hardest and began drinking heavily. No one blamed him for what happened, but he blamed himself. He dealt with his own guilt in his own way. I tried to encourage him to come to Church with me and seek the Lord. I figured he could bring us through this together. But Jake refused. I even tried to persuade him to see a therapistand do something that would help him get over his grief, but he wouldn't.

The more he drank, the more I turned to God. Shania, some people turn to God when tragedy hits, which is what he wants us to do. Others turn to whatever gives them the most comfort at that moment, whether it be alcohol, drugs, or sex. These things may offer temporary relief, but they never help. Jake was not only letting his drinking destroy him, but it almost destroyed our marriage.

He thought I blamed him for Jacob's death, and maybe I did at first. But I mostly blamed myself for planting that seed. I never realized what it meant in the Bible when it says, "Life and Death lies in the power of the tongue." I didn't know at the time that I was speaking death to my child, but once I realized that, it haunted me for a long time. I've since learned that God had bigger plans for our lives.

Jake's drinking got so bad that he couldn't keep a job. He would work only a few months here and a few weeks there, so naturally, he wasn't bringing in any money. The little bit he did make, he used it to buy liquor. But because of all the guilt I was feeling, I just couldn't give up on him. I used to say you can't kick a man when he's down. At that time, however, I was seeking counseling at my family's Church, and my mentor explained to me the importance of tough love. She told me that I was enabling Jake instead of helping him. She said that his actions could not only destroy our marriage but could destroy us both in the process. She explained that other negative behaviors come along with drinking, such as abuse, drunk driving, and immoral and illicit conduct. I thought about what she said for a few weeks and then gave Jake an ultimatum. It was either his drinking or me. Well, that just made his drinking worse because, in his mind, I had stopped believing in him.

One night I cried out to God like I've never done before. I asked him to give me the strength to either leave Jake or live with him. I hung in there with him, and just when I thought things couldn't get any worse, I found out that I was pregnant.

I didn't know if this was a blessing or a curse. The Devil kept telling me all the reasons why I should get rid of the baby. I worried that something bad was going to happen to this child, too. I worried the child would be born with some kind of defect because of Jake's drinking. I worried that we wouldn't be able to afford a child on one salary since, by that point, Jake was not working at all. I prayed to God to make this go away.

Then, one day, God put it in my spirit to talk to my mentor at the Church. So, I went to her and told her my situation. I asked her if she thought that God would forgive me if I chose not to keep the baby. She told me that God was a forgiving God and would forgive me, but would I be able to forgive myself, especially so soon after losing a child? Then she asked me what Jake's take on the situation was. The last thing I wanted to do was to get Jake's opinion. I felt that if he wasn't putting anything into our marriage, then he shouldn't have any say in what I decided to do. She still suggested that I talk it over with Jake before making any decisions and then take it to God in prayer. She called in some other church members, and they prayed with me that night and I fasted for three days.

A few days later, when I was in the shower, God spoke to me. He told me that this baby was the miracle that I'd been hoping for, and this child could save my marriage and Jake's life. I've been praying a long time for Jake's salvation, but this was the first time God has spoken to me. His voice was so clear that I turned off the shower and looked around to see where that voice came from. I grabbed a towel, rushed into our adjoining bedroom, and sat on my bed, waiting to hear from him again, but I guess he'd made his point clear enough. For the next few days, Jake hung around the house, which was unusual for him since he was always out somewhere, drinking with his drinking buddies. So, I decided this was a good time to approach him with my news.

When I told Jake that I was pregnant, he was so happy that he jumped up off his feet and lifted me up off the floor. I took this opportunity to use tough love on him once again. I looked him straight in his eyes and said, 'I'm not having this baby.' He looked into my eyes, and I could see his eyes tearing up. "What do you mean you're not having this baby? This is our second chance at having a family," Jake said, both angry and afraid. Tricia paused and then continued.

"What kind of family will that be? I asked him. With a father who's drunk and can't hold onto a job and a mother who's too afraid to love him because she is afraid that she might lose him too? A child deserves better than that, I told him, and guess what he said? He said he would stop drinking, but I knew he was making an impulsive decision to make me change my mind. He was so agitated with my decision that he questioned my faith. Shaina, would you believe that I was seeing a grown man cry like a baby? But I knew that I had to show him tough love, so I asked him what we had to offer our child.

How can we even think about bringing a child into this world if we're unable to give that child our best? He promised me that he would stop drinking. So now I knew that I had to play my cards carefully, and I told him to get himself together and come with me to Church.

That very next Sunday, he came to Church with me, and he's been going ever since." Tricia smiled and looked hopefully into Shaina's eyes.

"So, you guys had the baby?" Shania asked.

"Oh yeah, we had a beautiful daughter, Jalissa. Jake never even touched a drink from that night. He attended Church regularly, got saved, and joined an Alcoholics Anonymous program. God blessed us with two more children after that. We have three altogether, two girls and a boy. All I did was put my trust in God.

A few years later, Jake discovered that God had a calling in his life, and he became a pastor. His mission was to help others like himself. Right around the time Jake received his calling from God, and we were awarded a half million dollars from the American Automobile Industry, which went straight into our ministry. We brought this property and built Our Lady of Grace Church from the ground up. Jake is not only the Pastor of Our Lady of Grace Church, but he also operates the largest AA program in the city. Some nights before his AA meetings, Jake gets into his van and picks up drunks around the city. He brings them back to the Church for a hot meal and invites them to stay for the meetings. A few of them get saved every week.

So, you see, God has a way of turning a terrible situation into something good. He did it for us, and if you trust him, he will do it for you."

"I do trust him, Tricia," Shania said as she let her tears fall, "but you don't know the pain I feel every single day. It's a struggle just to get out of bed sometimes. I have this ache tugging at my heart that won't go away. Zach killed himself, and I don't have a clue why. Every day, I ask myself, 'Was it something I did?' My kids are suffering because of this, especially Zane. The boy is full of anger. I doubt if anything good can come out of this."

"I know how difficult it is to lose a loved one. It's the worst pain in the world, and I can only imagine how terrible it was for your son to find his dad like that. But there is a purpose to all of this, I promise. You may not know what it is now or even understand it, and you probably won't for a while. In the meantime, allow God to help you get through this. Thursday night is prayer night; why don't you come over to our Church Thursday and let our prayer partners pray with you."

"They'll do that for me?"

"Of course they will," Tricia replied.

"I just might take you up on that," Shania answered.

"Whenever you're ready, we are not going anywhere. We better be heading back before they call the hounds out for us,"

Tricia said, laughing as she reached for the bill.

"This is on me."

"Are you sure? I can pay for my own lunch." Shaina said.

"Of course, I'm sure. It's good to be the boss." They both laughed as they left the restaurant.

For the next few months, Shania tried to throw herself into her work so that she would be tired enough to fall fast asleep when she went to bed at night. Now that Trey and Zaria were back in school, Shania was anxious to get Zane back on track so she could rest. Zach had clouded every thought she had from the time she woke up in the morning to when she went to bed; he was always on her mind. She figured that the only way she could get her mind off him was to sleep, but despite her best efforts to tire herself out, most nights she laid awake, unable to sleep, but when she did, she dreamt about him. This nightly ritual left her constantly exhausted and irritable, and it seemed as if the dreams would never end. Some evenings, she would get on her knees and pray that she had no thoughts or dreams of Zach.

At the same time, Zane was demanding all her attention. She tried to summon the energy to help him work through his pain, but nothing seemed to help. He didn't want to go to school, he didn't want to hang out with his friends, and he didn't have any interest in being on his baseball team anymore; he didn't want to do anything. He just hung around the house and sulked. Shaina was exhausted from the emotional trauma. It took every ounce of energy she had to do even the smallest thing, such as getting out of bed, which she still couldn't seem to do on some days. The only thing that gave her the will to live was knowing she had three children to support. One day, when things got too much for her, she called Granny as she'd always done in times like this.

"Hi, Granny."

"Hey, baby, how's work going?"

"It's going. Everyone is going out of their way for me."

"That's a good thing considering all you've been through."

"I thought I would at least be able to sleep once I went back to work, but working has not helped. I'm more tired than before, and I still can't sleep. I'm too exhausted to do anything!"

"Give it some time. Sleep will come after a while. It wouldn't hurt to drink a glass of wine before you turn in; it'll help you sleep and get your mind off things. How are the kids holding up?"

"I don't know, Granny. Zane needs so much of my attention right now, and I don't have the energy to give it to him. I don't know what to do."

"It's no surprise that he needs your attention. The child's hurting just as much as you are. Remember, he's the one who discovered his dad."

"I know, but I barely have enough strength to pay attention to my own needs, much less his."

"If you don't find a way to give him the attention he needs, Shania, believe me; he'll get it somewhere else."

"Then there's Zaria; every other day, she calls to tell me that she can't sleep, can't eat, and can't concentrate on her schoolwork," Shania cried.

"Maybe she should take a semester off."

"And do what, Granny? Sit around the house and drive me crazy? It's bad enough I have to deal with Zane. They want so much from me right now, and I don't have anything left to give."

"What is wrong with you, Shania?" Granny snapped, taken aback at her granddaughter's callousness. "They need you, for heaven's sake. You're all they have left. Now you listen to me, and you listen carefully. Those kids just lost their dad just like you lost your husband and in the worst way possible. Now, if there ever was a time when you all needed to pull together and be there for one another, it's now. So, you better find a way to give those kids what they need. Get them some help, for Christ's sake, cause if you don't, believe me, you're gonna lose them too, one way or another. Reach out to them. Get your mind off yourself for a change. Do you hear what I'm saying to you, Shania?"

"Yes, Granny, I hear you, but…."

"Don't but me. You have good kids, Shania; don't let them go. You've got to do something. You to have to get them into counseling. I don't care if you to have to drive down to Zaria's school to get her to talk to somebody. What about Trey? How's he holding up?"

"Trey's keeping busy. His grades are good, and he's working. He's actually holding up pretty well."

"Well, I hope that is the case, but don't be too sure of that. He may be keeping it all in. Make sure to check up on him every now and then. At least the other two have sense enough to call for help, even if their mama is too preoccupied with herself to hear them."

"That's not fair, Granny,"

"I'm not trying to be fair. I'm trying to get you to see that those babies need you."

"Okay, Granny. I'm going to get help for them."

"Good, and while you're at it, get some for yourself. And don't forget to pray, Shania. Call on God. He's there for you."

"Call on God; He's there for you. That's all people keep telling me. Where was he when Zach needed him?" Shania hissed.

"He was right where he always is, waiting for Zach to call on him, just like he's waiting on you. Now, you can sit there and wallow in self-pity like Zach did, or you can call on him for help. The choice is yours. I'm going now. Call me if you need anything."

"I love you, Granny."

"I love you too, baby."

Granny hung up, feeling drained and saddened by their conversation. She wished she could do more to help. But she knew from experience that there was only so much she could do. Shania had to be the one to pull herself up. The only thing she could do was to pray for her.

Shania knew that Granny was right, but she felt tired all the time. She couldn't muster up the energy to do anything. She could not eat or sleep and had lost 25 pounds in less than three months. She knew that she had to do something for her kids' sake. The day after her conversation with Granny, she called Zaria and got her to agree to seek counseling on her campus.

Shania signed her and Zane up for counseling at Tricia and Jake's Church a week later. The sessions were held at one of the member's houses.

The counseling sessions seemed to be working. At first, they did family counseling until Zane agreed to go to counseling by himself, which allowed Shania to renew her one-on-one counseling.

She was at work one Tuesday evening when she noticed a few of her co-workers were in a rush to leave work. It dawned on her that they were in a hurry to leave every Tuesday. They didn't hang around and socialize like they did most nights. Then Shania heard one of her co-workers tell Tricia that she would see her later that evening. Out of curiosity, Shania asked her where they were hurrying off to. She told her that every Tuesday evening, from 6 to 8, the Church held 'Testimony Tuesdays.'

"What's Testimony Tuesday all about?" She asked.

"It's when our members and their guest share their stories about how God has blessed them or how they became saved. We started this night of praise to encourage each other and to bring us closer together. It helps to know that others have gone through the same things we are or have gone through. It also helps to keep down the spirit of gossip. Human nature as it is; sometimes, when people don't know your story, they will make one up for you. I'm ashamed to say it, but that's exactly what was happening at our Church, so Jake came up with this idea a few years ago. I tell you, the members love it. You saw for yourself how they rushed out of here today. Why don't you come by tonight? You would probably enjoy it."

"I think I will. Let me go home and change, and then I'll meet you there."

"You know where our church is, don't you?"

"Yes, it's the large building on the corner of Peachtree and 37th."

"That's it. See you there."

Our Lady of Grace took up the entire block. It was a large, beige, two-story, nondescript building that looked more like a hospital than a house of worship. When she entered, the Church was about one-fourth full. Most of the people who spoke at the meeting testified about how God had healed them or delivered them or about a family member recovering from alcohol or drug addictions. One person told how God healed her from a terminal illness.

Shania thought the meeting was inspiring, but she hoped to hear testimony about God delivering someone from circumstances like hers or Tricia's. She was still searching for answers, so she continued to go week after week, hoping to hear that kind of testimony. One Tuesday, after all the speakers finished giving their testimonies, Shania was walking toward the door when she overheard Tricia from behind her say to another of the attendees,

"I was hoping you would share your testimony with us this week, Sister Jones."

"Maybe next time, Sister Williams."

Shania wondered what her story was. Just then, Tricia spotted her as she was about to go out the door. She called out to her and introduced Lydia Jones. Tricia asked Shania if she could drive her home since she lived only a few blocks from her. Shania didn't mind. She was happy to have the company.

The entire left side of Lydia's face was permanently scarred as if she had been in a fire or some kind of accident. Even though she tried to conceal it with what looked like a half bottle of foundation, the scars were still noticeable. This made Shania even more curious to know her story.

"I noticed you've been to a few of our Testimony Tuesdays. Are you enjoying them?" Sister Jones asked after fastening her seat belt. Her mouth twisted slightly to the right side of her face as she talked.

"They're okay. To be honest, I was expecting the testimonies to be a little more," Shania answered.

"Really?" Sister Jones asked, puzzled.

"While I sympathize with these people, and I understand all they've been through, truth be told, the problems they're going through, they brought on themselves and probably could have been prevented. Personally, I was expecting someone to talk about something they had no control over, something similar to what Tricia Williams or I have been through. But all they talk about is how they overcame an addiction of some kind."

"Most addictions are a symptom of a larger problem. People usually turn to drugs or alcohol to cover up their pain because of something they've been through. In most cases, that something wasn't their fault. Did you know that Pastor Jake Williams is a recovering alcoholic?"

"Yes."

"Then you know the story about the accident with his son, which led to his alcohol addiction. He couldn't deal with the pain of losing his son." Lydia paused for a second to let the effect of what she was saying sink in. "Most people who tell their stories will only tell you how they overcame the addiction. That in itself is a victory. However, very few will talk about how or why their habits began in the first place. A lot of them came from dysfunctional families and were abused or raped, and some were even molested as children by the people who should have protected them. Some had parents who were substance abusers themselves. None of this was their fault, but these things are still too painful for a lot of people to talk about. They don't even want to think about it, much less talk about it. That's the reason most of them began using drugs or alcohol. Getting out of an addiction is a great accomplishment, especially drug addiction. It's a lifelong commitment. That's why many drug addicts don't recover- even if they do go to rehab, they eventually bounce back to their old habits. It is not easy to recover from an addiction, you know."

"I'm sorry; I don't mean to downplay anyone's pain. I guess I didn't think of it that way," Shania said, thinking she may have touched a nerve.

"Usually, when we're going through something painful, it's hard to relate to anyone else's story until you have heard something far worse than your own."

Shania nodded in agreement, embarrassed by what she had just said and even more embarrassed by what she was thinking. For the next several minutes, there was silence. All you could hear was the wind blowing from outside the car. As Shania reached to turn on the radio, Sister Jones put her hand on top of hers to stop her.

"So, tell me, what's your story, sister?" Lydia asked, breaking the awkward silence.

"I was going to ask you the same thing," Shania said.

"You first," Lydia responded.

Shania narrated the events of the past few months, how her husband had committed suicide several months earlier, and that their youngest son found him hanging in the bathroom. She also told her the most difficult part is that they will never know why because he didn't leave a note; not knowing why he did such a thing made it harder for her to adjust to the change. It was hard for her to accept the change in the first place.

"Sister Williams mentioned that to us one evening. She asked us to pray for the family, but I had no idea that it was your family."

"She asked y'all to pray for my family even though you didn't know us?"

"Oh yeah, that's the type of person Sister Williams is."

"Wow, she's some special lady."

"Yes, she is. And after all she's been through, she never let it change her."

"That's not easy. I'm trying not to be bitter, but I'm hurt and angry at Zach for doing this to us. I don't want to be, but I am. He didn't even think about what will happen to us. Knowing that what we had wasn't enough for him hurts so much. I don't even know what led him to suicide! Was it me? Was it someone else? Is there something I'm missing?"

"Please know it had nothing to do with you. Hurting people hurt people, and obviously, he was hurting. You may never know why he killed himself. I know you can't understand any of this right now, but God's word tells us, She said as she pointed toward the heavens, "that all things work together for good."

"You know Sister Jones, if I may," Shania asked.

"Of course."

"I grew up in the Church. My grandmother made sure we went to Church every Sunday, come rain or shine. That's how it was back then. Everybody went to some kind of house of worship. But as I got older, I'm ashamed to say I didn't go to Church much or take my children regularly. We just went on special occasions. We're good people, but we just couldn't find the time to give to God the way we should have. Now, people keep telling me to pray and seek him for help. I don't even know if God will want to help me after being away from him for so long."

"Of course, He will. We're all God's children, and he will never forsake us, just like we wouldn't give up on our children. By the Grace of God, I was able to survive the emotional pain that I went through. It took me a long time before I accepted Him completely. But when I did, I tell you He's the best thing that has ever happened to me."

"If he's the best thing that happened to you, why haven't you told your story yet?"

"Well, I think it's because I'm a little ashamed. It's like what we were talking about before. I'm still having a hard time forgiving myself."

"What is your story?" Shania pried.

"My story is similar to Sister Williams's, except I was the one driving under the influence and killed someone else's family. I also lost my entire family and almost didn't survive myself."

Shania was shocked at what she was hearing. She felt bad because she had wanted to hear a story that resembled her own. She couldn't imagine anything as bad as losing one's entire family. She wasn't prepared for what she heard next.

"We were on our way home from a friend's house. I hardly ever drove, but I had to that night. My husband, Michael, was visibly drunk, so everyone thought it would be best if I drove home since I only had one drink. What they didn't know was that I was addicted to pain pills. Michael was in the passenger's seat. My three kids, one being my six-month-old baby boy, were all in the back seat. I tried to turn and side-swiped another car, my car skidded, flipped over, and hit a tree. Everyone died on impact. They told me I was in a coma for four weeks. To this day, I don't know why God spared me. There were days when I wished He hadn't," she paused for a second, trying to get through the entire story.

"I had a difficult delivery with my second pregnancy. I couldn't even walk for two weeks; that's when the doctor gave me a pill prescription. When I was pregnant with my third child, I managed to stay off the pills during my pregnancy, but after I gave birth, I went right back on them. When my doctor noticed the signs of dependency, he stopped writing me prescriptions, so I found another doctor who would. All in all, I was able to function pretty well as long as I didn't drink while taking them. I don't know what made me take a drink the day of the accident. If I had known that I had to drive that night, I wouldn't have touched it."

"Did your husband know you were addicted to pain medication?" Shania asked.

"I never specifically told him, but I believe he did know. Occasionally, he would ask what I was taking medication for. I would always come up with an excuse for taking them. I thought I couldn't function without them. On this particular night, Michael had too much to drink, so I had no choice but to drive us home. Halfway to our house, he reached over to turn on the radio. I never drove with the radio on. It ruined my concentration, especially after I had popped a few pills, which was almost always the case. Michael always drove when we were together, so he didn't know this. Anyway, I reached over to turn the radio off, and he turned it back on. We were playing a game of tug of war with the radio knob when I realized that I had almost missed my turn. I tried to turn at the last moment," she cried. "My whole life changed in a split second."

Shania felt a wave of nausea overtake her. She had to swallow to keep from getting sick. She couldn't imagine losing her entire family, forgetting being the one responsible for all their deaths. She was visibly shaken by what she had just heard. It felt surreal coming from a woman as humble as the one sitting next to her. It was hard to accept that such a horrible thing could happen to such a nice person. She felt ashamed about the fact that she even wanted to hear someone else's life story. After digesting what she had just heard, Shania told her how sorry she was for being so insensitive.

"You were just saying what you were feeling. We all do that sometimes. Just remember there is always someone who has gone through something worse than you."

"Is that how you found God? Through your suffering?"

"Well, yes and no. He found me. Have you heard about our prayer partners?"

"Yes, Tricia mentioned it to me. She said they get together on Thursday nights and pray together."

"In addition to their Thursday night prayer service, some members, mostly the older ones, get together with members from other churches, and they pray for the sick and shut-ins. They also go out to hospitals and prisons and pray for non-believers. Well, unbeknown to me, while I was in a coma, they came by the hospital several times and prayed for me. The funny thing was that I could hear voices a few times when I was in a coma. I distinctly remember hearing, 'You will live and not die.'

After I came out of the coma and was well enough, they placed me under arrest and charged me with four counts of vehicular manslaughter, driving while under the influence, and a few other charges. They placed a police officer at my door, and as soon as they thought I was well enough to be moved, I was transferred to the prison hospital. They put me on a suicide watch because they knew that I had no will or desire to live without my family. I was unable to post bail, and I couldn't ask my family for help, so I was prepared to stay there until my trial. That's when I started receiving literature and a Bible from Our Lady of Grace.

One Sunday afternoon, Sister Williams and a few members came to the prison and posted a request to visit me. They knew about my accident because they visited me in the hospital and they wanted to pray with me.When they heard about the charges, they held all-night prayer services outside the prison. A few weeks later, they posted my bail and got an attorney to represent me through a pro bono case. Long story short, my charges were reduced, and eventually, I was acquitted. It was determined that the other driver was driving without a license and was at fault. He had side-swiped my car instead of being the other way around. To this day, I don't know why the prayer partners singled me out, but I know it had to be by the Grace of God that I was given a second chance. I can't begin to tell you how grateful I am. I haven't touched a pill or a drink since then. Praise God."

"Wow, now that's some testimony. And you're not ready to sit yet?"

"I share my story almost every week at our women's ministry. I just haven't told it outright on Testimony Tuesday."

"They also have a Women's ministry?" Shania asked, surprised.

"Yes, we have a women's ministry and a men's ministry, too. They meet once a week. There are new members coming in all the time, and it helps them feel comfortable in our Church. We started the women's ministry to encourage women to open up and let God work through us to help them. Some women have problems that are often related to the men in their lives, whether it's their fathers, husbands, or boyfriends. Most of them feel more comfortable talking to a woman.

It was a while before we realized that our brothers also needed guidance. Their issues are very different from ours. Many of them come from broken homes where their mothers had to be both a mother and a father. Our veteran brothers take them under their wings and teach them what the Bible says about the role of the husband, father, and provider. We want both the women and men in our Church to be in an environment where they can open up and have honest dialogues about what they have been through in their lives and share what they have learned.

We also emphasize the importance of the family worshiping together; as the saying goes, 'a family who prays together stays together.' Jake and Tricia Williams not only run a church but have also built a slew of programs and resources that have helped to bless the entire community."

"That's impressive. She told me about some of their programs," Shania said as she pulled up to Lydia's house. "Well, here we are."

"Have you been to any of our Sunday services?" Lydia asked, not making any attempt to leave the car.

"No, I haven't."

"Great guest speakers from some of the largest churches in the country come to speak at our Church. This Sunday, our speaker is an Atlanta native, Tony Bradford. He moved out west to pastor a mega church out there. He's a well-known Pastor. You should come and check him out," Lydia said as she gave Shania a flyer for Sunday's service.

"Besides, I could use a ride. My number is on the back," She added as she opened the car door.

"Let me think about it. I'll give you a call later in the week.

She called Granny that night and told her about Testimony Tuesdays and meeting Lydia Jones. She told her how Sister Lydia's story had touched her heart and that she was invited to their service on Sunday. She asked Granny to come with her, but Granny declined, saying that she didn't like to miss Sunday services at her Church unless she was sick. Shania tried to convince her that she would like Our Lady of Grace because of their outreach and community service. Granny said that was no surprise any good church worth its weight had to have some type of involvement with the people in their community. She said she wasn't comfortable at these large megachurches because they felt too impersonal for her liking. But Granny was happy because she hadn't heard Shania that excited about anything in a long time. She was glad that Shania was thinking about going back to Church. She suggested she take Zane with her. She hoped it would help bring a change in both of their lives.

Shania called Lydia a few days later to let her know she would pick her up for Church on Sunday.

Shania, Zane, and Lydia arrived just as the service was about to begin. The main chapel seated over five thousand people in theatre-style seats with large, comfortable chairs. There was a gorgeous massive chandelier in the center of the main chapel; they also had several plasma monitors placed around the Church. There were two stages; the center stage had a lectern kept in the center and a small table with a glass and a pitcher of water on the left side for the speaker. The other stage was for the band and the choir. Next to the chapel were the restrooms and the secretary's office.

On the second floor was a balcony that seated an additional 1,000 people. There was a family room with two plasma monitors where parents could sit with their children and listen to the services, and there was also a restroom. Next to the family room were two smaller rooms, which were where their youth bible study and their men and women ministries were held.

The pastor's office was also on the second floor. In the basement was another restroom, a large kitchen with all the latest appliances, and a huge dining room with plasma monitors in each corner.

The service was packed. Shania could feel the energy vibrating throughout the whole building. This was the first time she had attended a Sunday service at Our Lady of Grace, and she was surprised to see the room almost full. She thought she would have to sit on the balcony since they were a little late, but Lydia directed her to the front, where seats were reserved for her, the other ushers, and their guests.

The speaker's message was about forgiveness. Shania felt his eyes on her as if the young minister was speaking directly to her.

"Good morning, brothers and sisters," the young, energetic minister addressed the crowd in a deep voice.

"I said good morning, brothers and sisters," he said again, this time adding a little bass for emphasis as if his voice wasn't deep enough the first time.

"Good morning!" the crowd answered.

"That's what I'm talking about. It's always a good morning when we make our way into the Lord's house. Amen?"

"Amen," everyone chimed.

"I'm glad to be back home in Atlanta. I'm going to talk to you this morning about forgiveness. Forgiving someone is not an easy thing to do. We've all been unforgiving at some point in our lives, and it's okay. It's human nature to have resentment towards someone who has hurt us. It's hard to forgive sometimes. It's even harder to forgive if that person is a close confidant, friend, or family member. Why? Because we had faith in that person. We thought we could trust them.

Now, I'm not saying we should continue to allow them to hurt us, but when we are hurt or wronged by someone, we should find it in our hearts to forgive them and move on. Why am I saying that we should forgive them? Because that's what our Father God wants us to do. He tells us to be followers of our Lord Jesus. Christ Jesus forgave right up to his time of death. When he was about to be crucified, he looked to his left and right and said, 'Father, forgive them, for they know not what they do.' He knew that they were imperfect. And who knows better than him? Do you claim to be greater than Jesus? No, right- so if he forgave everyone all his life, who are you to hold a grudge?

God does not want us to forgive people for His sake or even for the sake of another person. He wants us to forgive them for our sake. People don't realize that it's for our benefit to forgive and move on. When we forgive someone, we are freeing ourselves from reliving the hurt and pain we've been through. We release our bodies from the stress caused by worrying and contemplating evil for evil. By forgiving them, we open up a way to allow God to handle things. You see, as long as we hold on to unforgiveness and try to figure out a way to get even, God is not going to touch it. It's not our job to punish anyone who has hurt us. It's not even our job to judge that person. God's word tells us not to judge one another. He says, 'Judge not lest ye be judged.' We don't know what those other people have been through to cause them to act the way they do.

It's important for us to forgive so we can move on and live healthy and productive lives. We must learn to use up the energy that it takes to be angry with someone to do something positive to help others. Brothers and sisters, don't waste time and energy being angry and vengeful- leave that to God. 'Vengeance is mine, saith the Lord.' More than likely, the person you're angry at doesn't even care that you're angry at them. They may not even remember what they did that made you angry.

The Bible is God's roadmap to where we want to go and how God is going to help get us there. It not only has all the answers for what we will go through in life, but it also gives us stories and examples that will help us in all areas of our lives.

Don't dwell on what someone has done to you in the past. Keep moving forward. The Bible tells us to 'let go of yesterday.' It says, 'Forget those things which are behind and reach forth for which is before us.' Do not look back at our past; look forward. God has greater things in store for us.

Before we close with prayer, let us all stand. I want everyone to hold the hand of the person next to them and close your eyes. Now, I want you to call out the name of the person or persons who have hurt you. Call out the names of those who have betrayed you and ask God to give you the power to forgive them." He paused as they called out names.

"That's right; scream out their names," he continued. "Tell them that you forgive them." He ended the service with a prayer.

Shania let out a deep breath as she felt a heavy load lift off her shoulders. Her face was tear-stricken, but her heart was light. She didn't realize how good forgiveness felt until that moment. She knew she was only hurting her children by holding on to her resentment toward Zach. She was relieved to be able to let it go. She called Granny that night and told her all about the service.

Shania invited Zane to attend Church with her again the following Sunday. At first, he declined. Each week, she would tell him about the service and about the wonderful message she received. One Sunday, he decided to go with her again. The message delivered that Sunday was just as powerful and inspiring as the first one they heard. The two of them began to attend Sunday services regularly from that point on.

Sunday evenings, she couldn't wait to call Granny to tell her what she learned that week. She pleaded with Granny to come with her, but Granny would always say that she had her own Church to attend.

Shania's spirituality grew day by day. She began reading and studying the Bible daily. Within a few months, Shania became a member of the Church. She brought inspirational CDs to listen to in her car and DVDs to watch at home, and she attended all the special events sponsored by the Church and heard some of the most famous evangelists speak.

Although Zane accompanied his mother to Church each week, he didn't have the same enthusiasm as she had. He did find some comfort in the sermons but wasn't interested in joining any of their programs.

After a year, Shania thought it was time for her to be baptized, so she spoke to Pastor Williams about her decision. He instructed her that she had to attend Bible classes first in preparation for her baptism. She did as she was instructed. She was fascinated with many of the stories in the Bible, especially the stories about women. These stories gave her the inspiration and strength she needed.

She told Granny that she wanted her to be there for her big day. Although Granny was not comfortable in large mega churches, her excitement that her granddaughter would finally be giving her life to the Lord allowed her to put her feelings aside. She told Shania how proud she was of her and that she wouldn't miss her baptism for anything in the world.

Zane, Granny, and her friend Betty attended the ceremony. All the candidates for the baptism had to wear all white. Granny strutted proudly into the Church, wearing her bright hot pink suit and a big hot pink hat with her white pumps and matching bag, with Zane and Betty in tow. Granny had prayed for years for all her children's and grandchildren's salvation. Shania was the only one other than her son Gary to make that commitment. Granny's chest poked out with pride because she knew she had raised Shania right.

Granny baked her famous bread pudding with banana sauce for dinner afterward and carried it in a large shopping bag. Zane offered to carry the dessert for her, but she insisted on taking it herself as she held her head high.

"Lord, Shania, look at all these folks," Granny said, taking it all in. "And look at all those big-screen TVs, Betty. With all these folks tithing, I guess they can afford it."

"They're monitors, Granny, so the congregation can see and hear the service from anywhere in the Church. It's not about the material things."

"You wouldn't know that by the looks of things. Good Lord, look at that huge crystal chandelier up there," Granny whispered as she nudged her friend.

"Granny, you wouldn't be passing judgment if you knew how much this Church has done for the neighborhood with its community service and outreach programs. They may take in a lot, but they give back way more than they take in."

"I guess you got a point there," Granny said as she looked around, feeling a little ashamed. "How come I don't see a cross anywhere in this church?"

"Because this is an interfaith church and not a Baptist or Catholic Church. People of all faiths are welcome here. Besides, they don't display idols."

"Idols? Hmm…" she said, "In my day, the cross was a way of keeping the Devil out," Granny replied; just then, the service began.

Pastor Jake Williams explained to them the responsibilities that come with giving themselves to the Lord. He gave them his blessings. After the service was over, the baptismal candidates were asked to come up to the front after they got changed. He said a few words to each of them as he rubbed anointing oil on their heads.

He then allowed the families who wished to take pictures to come up to the front. Then he began the baptism. Granny was so happy she cried with joy. She got her camera from her pocketbook and rushed to the front to take pictures of her granddaughter being submerged in water. She left her bag with her dessert on her chair as she called for

Zane to join her. Afterward, they went back to their seats while they waited for Shania to change.

Shania introduced Sister and Pastor Williams to Granny, and then they all took pictures together. Sister Williams asked Granny if she was going to stay for dinner. Granny said, "Absolutely." Then she asked Zane to fetch her shopping bag with her bread pudding in it.

"I made a bread pudding with a nice banana sauce for dessert," she said as she offered Sister Williams the huge shopping bag.

"Oh, that wasn't necessary, Sister Atkins. We had everything catered, including dessert."

"You mean with all these church folk here, you all had to cater food?"

Shania looked at Granny, embarrassed, and said, "Granny, folks here are too busy to worry about cooking. The Church is nice enough to honor us and our families with a nice dinner on our special day. We appreciate you all going out of your way, Sister Williams."

"Yes, we do appreciate it, Sister. If you all don't have any use for the bread pudding, then take it home for your family because I made one for our family, too," she said, clearly offended.

"Of course, we'll use it, Sister Atkins. I don't know anyone who doesn't like bread pudding."

"Now we're talking." Granny chuckled, and then she turned and winked at Betty before following Sister Williams to the dining room for supper.

Chapter Five
Tragedy Strikes Twice

Our Lady of Grace had a lot of activities for teens. They had an arts and crafts program for the younger teens and a baseball team where the teams played against other churches. They had an awesome teen choir, and they hired a voice coach to work with them. After much encouragement from Shania, Zane joined the baseball team and began to take Bible studies with some of the teens his age. He was excited to meet new friends who shared his interest. He learned the importance of giving back, which eventually led him to sign up as a mentor to some of the younger members. He enjoyed working with the younger ones. He took a lot of pride in his 'big brother role.' He seemed to be happier than he had been since Zach's death.

As Shania watched the change in her son, she was so happy with her decision to join the church. She regretted her and Zach's decision not to bring their children up in church. She wondered if things between them could have been different if they had attended church regularly. Putting that aside, she was pleased with her and Zane's decision. She was looking forward to the day that he took the plunge as she had.

Several months later, Zane came home from school with a long face. He sat on the sofa, staring into space.

"What's wrong, Zane?" Shania asked.

"Nothing," he answered as he continued staring.

Shania was a little concerned since she had seen Zach do this same thing many times. She decided to wait for him to tell her what was going on instead of pushing him. About 15 minutes later, he opened up to her.

"Mom, Do you remember when I told you we had to write a paper about one of our worst experiences in life for our health class?"

"Yeah."

"Well, I wrote that my worst experience was finding my father dead and how he committed suicide. At first, some of my classmates didn't believe me. Then Mr. Robinson told them that it was true and that was why I was absent from school for a while last year. Now, some of them are saying that someone must have killed my dad and made it look like a suicide because black people don't commit suicide. Other kids are saying that it's not true. The class got into a big discussion about it, so Mr. Robinson gave everyone an assignment on the topic. He said those who believe that African Americans don't commit suicide have to research their facts and write a report about why they believe that. Those who believe that anyone, regardless of race, is capable of committing suicide must write a report supporting their point of view. Everyone must present statistics on the suicide rate for at least three different races; one of them must be African American. He wants the class to begin working on the assignment next week. This made me so upset, and I told him that I didn't appreciate him giving an assignment on the circumstances of my father's death. He said that people need to learn not to make generalizations without any knowledge of what they're saying. Then, he told me that he wanted me to write a different assignment from the others. He said that our follow-up assignment was going to be on how we got through that experience. And he wants just me to write about how I'm coping with my father's death. I can't write that, Mom; I'm barely coping!"

"You are coping, Zane. Look at where you're at now and where you were last year when you found your dad. You were so angry and full of resentment. You didn't want to go back to school, hang out with your friends, go to counseling, or do anything. Now you're going to church, you joined some of their activities, and you're making new friends. Most of all, you're able to hold your head up and talk about it. You were even able to write an entire paper about it, Zane."

"That wasn't by choice. I had to write about my worst experience, and I was just being honest."

"Yeah, but you could have written about an experience a little less close to home if you wanted to. The point is that you are coping with your father's death pretty well. Your paper may help someone else when you share your truth."

"I don't know. I think it's the church that's helping me to cope."

"Well, there you go. Write about that."

"That's not a paper's worth, Mom."

"Once you begin writing, more things will come to you. Anyone living in pain or despair can commit suicide. The statistics may not be as high for African Americans as it is for others. But I tell you one thing: blacks commit suicide every day when they take or sell drugs or when they do drive-bys, and when they drink and drive. Self-destructive behavior in black communities is high and is a form of suicide, whether we believe it or not. When blacks are in pain and despair, we, as a whole, don't reach out for help as much as other races do. Instead, many reach for drugs, alcohol, or gang-related activities, all of which are self-destructive."

"You act like only African Americans deal drugs or are in gangs. Other races do drugs and are in gangs, too, Ma."

"You're absolutely right. Drugs and gangs are rampant in this country. It's the same thing with suicide; anyone could be in enough pain to want to end it, regardless of their race."

"Do you think Dad was in some sort of pain?"

"I know he was, and he has been for some time."

"Is that why he stopped doing things with us?"

"Unfortunately, yes. Your father had been through a lot throughout his life, and instead of letting go of the past, he held on to it and relived it over and over. That's why it's important to forgive and move on. We can't hold on to things that happened in the past because they will haunt us sooner or later."

"You said he was in pain for a long time. Was he in pain before you married him?"

"I believe he was."

"Then why did you marry him? You didn't know that it would be like this, did you?"

"No, I didn't know it would end up like this. But if I hadn't married your father, I wouldn't have had you guys. Your father suffered from depression. Depression can do terrible things to people, physically and mentally. Zach's best friend was killed when they were in the Army, and he never fully recovered from that."

'That's why I'm never going to go into the Military. Trey said that Dad had a rough childhood, and that's why he was messed up in the head."

"He lost his father at an early age."

"Didn't you lose your mother when you were growing up? That's why Granny had to raise you and Aunt Cassandra, right?

"Yes, that's right."

"You turned out okay. Besides, Dad still had his mother. I think that losing a mother is worse than losing a father."

"Losing any parent is hard. Death affects each person differently. Your dad's situation was a little more complicated than most. One day, we're going to sit down and talk about things in depth."

"We don't have to, Mom. Trey already told me about Dad's family and that Dad's father committed suicide, too."

"Trey? How does he know about that?"

"Trey is the oldest, Mom; he knows a lot about Dad. You know he spent a lot of time talking with Uncle Ted, and he told Trey about Dad."

"Did he really?" Shania said, a little concerned.

"Yep. Mom, I have some homework to do."

"Zane, I am proud of you, baby."

"You're proud of me for what?"

"For not giving up. You've been through a lot. Your father's death had a greater impact on you than it did on Trey and Zaria. Yet, you're still pressing on. Keep up the good work, baby."

Zane gave his mother a long, confused look, then said, "Thanks, Mom," and then he left the room.

Zane was more than halfway through his junior year in high school, and he seemed to be holding his own, considering all that he's been through. Then, suddenly, he began to express his unhappiness with his school and expressed that he didn't want to return next year. Shania was concerned because his school was the best school out of the three high schools in their district. She did as Granny reminded her to do; she took it to God and asked for His guidance.

It was right after Zane received the writing assignment from his teacher that he began to distance himself from his classmates. Just being around them reminded him of his father's suicide. Then, a few weeks before school ended, Zane went to his mother and pleaded with her not to send him back there for the next school term.

"Mom, please don't make me go back to Carter."

"Zane, what happened so bad that you don't want to go back to your school? Did someone do something to you?"

"No, Mom, no one did anything to me. It's just not the same since Dad died. It's like everyone is looking at me with pity or something."

"You just began going there when your dad died. A lot of your friends don't even attend the same school, except for Keyshawn and Troy. Is everything okay with them? They don't come around as much as they used to," Shania asked, trying to get an edge on what was going through Zane's mind.

"Yeah, everything's cool with them. Troy's busy with school and basketball stuff, and Keyshawn has a girlfriend who takes up a lot of his time."

"A girlfriend? Do I detect a little jealousy?"

No. Seriously, Mom, I was thinking of going to that Christian School that Pastor Jake told us about."

"What Christian School? Since when have you been interested in going to a Christian School?" Shania asked, unable to hide her surprise.

"A few fellows on the baseball team are thinking about transferring there. Everyone there is Christian. Pastor Jake said that the teens there don't have the same pressures that they have in public schools."

"Really?"

"Yeah. They're having an open house this Friday evening, and I'm thinking about checking it out."

"Sounds like a good idea. Do you mind if I go with you?"

"No if you don't mind hanging out with the fellows and me. They're going with me."

"I don't have a problem with that, Zane. I just want to see for myself what this school has to offer. I also want to look into the tuition and see if it's doable."

"Pastor Jake said that they have scholarships and some sort of financial aid that we can apply for. He gave me some brochures. Here, Mom." He said as he handed the brochures to her. "I just hope we can afford it."

"If you're really serious about this, then we can make it happen. Besides, my job is to set up a trust fund for your education."

"Really, how come you never told me this?

"Because it's supposed to be for college, but I think it's enough to do both."

"But you still could've told me about the fund, Mom. Did they set up anything for Trey and Zaria?"

"No, because they're already in college," she answered while flipping through the pamphlet. "I'll read this over before Friday."

Shania was impressed by what she read and with what she saw when she visited All Saints Christian High School. She was surprised to see that their curriculum surpassed the curriculum at Zane's High School. In addition to their regular studies, it was mandated that all students take a course in religious studies, which consisted of the study of all the religions in the world. Since this was a four-year course, Zane would have to make up the years he missed in summer school. The tuition was affordable, they offered financial aid to children of single parents, and they took in hardship cases for those who were unable to pay the full amount.

She met with Jake to see what he could tell her about the school. He told her that a few of the member kids went there, and from what he learned, the school had a great reputation.

Shania explained to Zane that if he was to attend this school, he had to buckle down and be prepared to do some hard work. She also told him that he had to be sure that this was what he wanted because once she signed the papers, there would be no turning back. Zane said that he was ready for a change.

That summer, Zane began attending religious studies. He and his new friends were excited about what they were learning. Even though he attended Bible study at the church, they only touched the surface of what he was learning in summer school. He shared with her and Granny what he had learned. Shania was happy to see Zane's excitement. She hasn't seen him this excited about anything since he joined the Little League when he was in elementary school. She was glad of his choice.

Granny was glad that he was learning about God. She just wished Shania would have taken them to church sooner.

Shania was happy that they were heading in the right direction by learning to put God first in everything. The counseling they both received at the church was Godsend. Zane was learning how to go to God in prayer whenever he had a problem. He learned the correct way to pray and to believe that his prayers would be answered. Shania noticed that he was happier and less depressed these days.

Zane said that he was thinking about getting his Master of Divinity after he graduates from college. Shania did her best to conceal her surprise and her excitement. She knew from experience that at this age, there was a good chance that he would change his mind a few times. However, she encouraged him to research colleges that offer a bachelor's in theology or a seminar school that focuses on graduate programs. Zane told her that although he had time, he had already begun his research.

Lydia took Shania under her wing and taught her the importance of building a strong relationship with God. They soon formed a special bond. Shania began to read her Bible more. Lydia helped her to navigate the chapters that she had trouble understanding. As her knowledge of the word grew, Lydia invited Shania to work with her in the women's ministry. In addition to assisting her in setting up the ministry, she helped to recruit new members.

Shania was finally beginning to feel somewhat like her old self again. She now had a purpose. She began sleeping better. Her dreams were less frequent and not as dark. She still dreamt about Zach, but she began dreaming more and more about their younger years together. Things were finally beginning to look up for the Taylor family.

A year after Zach's death, Trey graduated from Gary's alma mater, Clark University in Atlanta. After his graduation ceremony, the family took him to dinner at Chris Ruth's Steakhouse to celebrate. Trey chose this as a way of including his father in his celebration. Granny and Gary each gave Trey a $100 gift certificate. Shania offered to pay for a vacation anywhere he wanted to go, but he turned down the offer. He knew his mother was trying to keep up with all the other parents, but he was concerned about their finances now that his father was gone.

Trey moved back home, and he found a job at a bank; however, he was not happy. He was anxious because he was unable to find a job in his field. It seemed like every position that he applied for required someone with experience. Trey increasingly became more and more anxious. He was used to doing something he loved. Shania tried to explain to him the importance of patience.

Zaria brought her grades up and was able to keep her scholarship. Her dorm needed a Residence Assistant for the summer, so she applied and got the position. She was able to remain in her dorm for the summer, free of charge, while she took a few summer classes to keep her grades on point. Shania wished that Zach was there to see how well their children were doing. She knew that he would have been proud of them. She thanked God once again for his grace and mercy and for helping her get her family back on track. In fact, she was amazed at how well they were doing in the short time since Zach's death. She knew that without God, they could not have come this far, and for that, she was grateful.

One Saturday afternoon, Shania was sitting on the sofa in her family room, catching up on her Bible reading, when Trey walked in and sat down next to her. He waited for her to look up from her reading and then asked, "Mom, can I talk to you for a minute?"

"Sure, you can, baby," she replied as she closed her Bible.

"You know that I haven't been able to find a job that I like since I graduated, so I was thinking about joining the Air Force."

"The Air Force?" Shania said as she sat up straight. "Trey, you just graduated a few months ago. A lot of college graduates are having trouble finding jobs in their fields. It takes time; no one's pressuring you.

"I know, Mom. But I feel like I'm wasting my time working at the bank. I want to get my master's in business management. The government will help pay for it once I join the Air Force. It will improve my chances of getting a decent job."

"The Air Force is not an option, Trey," Shania said, shaking her head no.

"Why not, Mom? What's the big deal?"

"The big deal is that we didn't pay for you to go to college, only for you to end up in the military."

"I want to do something for my country."

"Then volunteer. There are a lot of programs out there that will allow you to help people right here in this country. There's too much going on in the Middle East; this is not the time to join the Air Force," Shania said in a high-pitched voice.

"This is something I really want to do."

"No way. We had already lost two men to war. I can't risk losing you too."

"What are you talking about? We didn't lose anyone to war."

"I'm talking about your father and your grandfather."

"They were casualties of their minds, Mom. Not war."

"Their deaths were the direct result of war."

"Come on, Mom. Grandpa, I can understand. A lot of people came back messed up from Vietnam. But Dad's head was screwed up way before he went into the Army. Uncle Ted told me how he freaked when Grandpa died, and he never fully recovered. His problems began before he joined the military. He also told me that Dad was adopted. Did you know that, Mom?"

"Yes, your grandmother told me."

"Did you know that Uncle Ted and Aunt Rhonda are Grandpa and Grandma's natural children?"

"Yes. A lot of times, couples have children right after they adopt."

"Dad never felt like he belonged."

"Your grandmother made sure she treated all her kids the same."

"Grandma didn't tell him that he was adopted until after Grandpa died. She didn't know that his father had already told him and made him keep it a secret. Can you imagine what it was like for him to have to keep that secret for all those years?" Trey asked.

"People weren't as open about things back then as they are now. Your Grandpa did what he thought was right. He didn't want to upset your grandmother."

"I know; Uncle Ted told me."

"When did Uncle Ted tell you all of this?"

"Right after Dad died. Did Dad ever try to find his real parents?"

"No, he didn't want to upset his mother. But what does any of this have to do with you joining the Air Force, Trey?"

"You're the one who brought up Dad and Grandpa."

"Yes, because I don't want you to fall into the same generational curse that your father did."

"Oh, come on, Mom; you don't believe that bull crap, do you?"

"You better watch how you talk to me, Zachary. I don't care how grown you think you are." She used his proper name to let him know that she was serious.

"Sorry, Mom. But you're going to church, and you're talking about curses. What's that about?"

"I'm talking about generational curses, bad habits, and characteristics we subconsciously pick up from our parents. Whether you realize it or not, that's probably why you want to join the Air Force."

"I want to join the Air Force because I can't find my dream job."

"If you're not happy, I can ask some folks at the church if you can work there. They're always hiring young people."

"No, thank you, Mom. That's your thing."

"My mind is made up," Trey said as he stood up for emphasis. "You know, Mom. Granny was right. She said that you'd be upset when I told you about my plans."

"You told Granny about your plans before you told me?"

"Mom, I know how you are. So, I went to Granny to get some advice on how to tell you."

"And what did she say, other than 'I would be upset'?"

"She said that I'm a man now and, at the end of the day, whatever decision I make is entirely up to me. She said that everyone else would just have to live with it."

'That sounds like something she would say. Look, Trey, all I ask is that you think about it for a few days before you make that decision, okay? Would you do that for me, please?" she asked, clearly upset.

"Okay, I'll think about it, but I doubt I'll change my mind."

"Fair enough."

Shania was so worried after hearing Trey's news that she could barely sleep that night. She was afraid that Trey's joining the military would have the same effect on him as it had on Zach. The next morning, she was still so upset and depressed that she couldn't get out of bed, so she decided to take a mental health day. It's just like Granny to take everyone's side against me, she thought to herself. Shania never liked to confront Granny, but she knew that she had to tell her how she felt about her meddling in her family's affairs.

Shania sat at the kitchen counter with a cup of coffee. She needed to get her thoughts together before she called Granny. Maybe after she hears my side, she will understand why I don't want Trey to go into the military. Then she could explain this to him. Kids his age always listen to others before they listen to their parents, she thought as she dialed her number.

"Good morning, Granny."

"Good morning, baby. I'm surprised to hear from you this early in the day."

"I stayed home from work today."

"Oh? Are you feeling under the weather this morning?"

"No, I'm okay. I needed to take a mental health day."

"A mental health day?" Granny laughed. "Lord, that's a new one on me."

"Trey told me about his plans to join the Air Force," Shania said, deciding to get right to the point.

"So that's why you needed to take a mental health day? Because Trey wants to join the Air Force?"

"Yes, Granny. I'm very upset about his decision. And I'm more upset that he talked to you about it before talking to me."

"Why would you be upset because he talked to me? What kind of sense does that make? It's not like I'm a stranger."

"I'm his mother, Granny. You should have told him to discuss it with me first," Shania snapped, trying to remain calm.

"Trey came to me and asked if he could talk to me about something. What would I look like, telling a grown man to talk to his mama first? You're being ridiculous, you know that?"

"I don't think I'm being ridiculous, Granny. You always take everyone else's side against me."

"It's not a matter of taking sides, Shania. Trey is 22 years old, and he has the right to talk to whomever he chooses."

"He wants to go into the military, Granny. I don't think that's a wise choice."

"It may not be, but it's his choice to make. He has to make his own mistakes in life, Shania. I didn't think it was wise for you to get married when you were his age, but you chose to do it anyway."

"I'm not talking about me, Granny. Besides, I was more mature than Trey was at his age."

"Were you?"

"Yes, I was. Granny, I need you to back me on this. There's a war going on in the Middle East, or have you forgotten? Look at what the after-effects of the military did to Zach and his father."

"Your son wants to show his support for his country, just like his father and grandfather chose to do. That's a decision he, and he alone, has the right to make."

"Your influence doesn't help any."

"What influence? The boy came to me to tell me his decision. His mind was made up long before he got here."

"But you should have…."

"Should have what?" Granny said, cutting her off before she could finish her sentence. "I'm not going to keep going around this merry-go-round with you, Shania. You raised an intelligent young man who knows what he wants out of life. Like it or not, he's going to do what his heart tells him to do. The more you protest, the more determined he'll be. That's all I got to say on the matter." She hung up the phone without saying goodbye.

After Granny hung up, Shania threw the cordless phone across the room, laid her head on the counter, and began to cry uncontrollably.

"Zach, how could you be so selfish and leave us like this?" she cried. "Those kids are at the ages in their lives where they need their father, especially the boys. Your son, your namesake, wants to make the biggest decision of his life, and I don't know how to help him. Why did you give up on yourself, Zach? Why did you give up on us?"

A few days later, Shania was able to pull herself together and think logically about the situation. She came to the conclusion that Granny was right. If she didn't handle things delicately, Trey would be more determined to go into the Air Force. She prayed about it and decided to leave it in God's hands.

The conversation about Trey was the last that Shania had with Granny. Two weeks later, Shania got the call she'd been dreading for most of her life. Her uncle Gary called to tell her that Granny died in her sleep.

Trey and Zane were sound asleep in their separate bedrooms when they heard their mother's gut-wrenching screams. They both jumped up and ran towards their mother's room. Zane froze. He stopped short of entering the room. He could still envision his father hanging from the shower in the bathroom. Trey nudged him aside and went in. Zane reluctantly followed behind him.

"What's wrong, Mom?" Trey asked nervously.

"Granny's gone," she cried.

"You mean she's dead?" Zane asked from behind Trey as he walked up to his mother's bed.

"Yeah, Uncle Gary called and said that he found her dead when he went in to wake her up this morning. Apparently, she died in her sleep."

Zane dropped to his knees beside his mother's bed and sobbed loudly. Shania was too distraught to comfort her son. She could not imagine her life without her grandmother. Shania was beside herself with grief and guilt. Trey and Zane tried to console her, but once they realized that she was inconsolable, Trey thought it was best to leave her alone for a while.

A few hours later, they tried to enter her bedroom but found her door locked. They knocked and pleaded with her to open the door. Although she wouldn't answer, they could hear her crying from outside the door. Zane was afraid for his mother, so he called Pastor Williams at the church. Jake and Tricia Williams picked up Lydia, and they rushed over as fast as they could.

"We came over as soon as we got your message. Where is she?" Tricia asked.

"She locked herself in her bedroom. She's been in there all day. My uncle Gary called, he told her that Granny died this morning, and now she's freaking out," Zane cried.

"I'll show you to her room," Trey said, leading the way.

They could hear Shania moaning from outside her bedroom door. It took some coaxing and convincing before she opened her bedroom door. She fell into Tricia's arms, crying. Lydia patted her back while trying to calm her down.

"She's gone, Sister Williams; my Granny's gone. She left me."

"I know, Sister. Your Granny was tired. Her job was finished here, and now she's gone to be with the Lord."

"I never got a chance to apologize to her and tell her how much I loved her."

"She knew. Your Granny knew how much you loved her; believe me."

"You don't understand. Granny and I had some words two weeks ago, and we haven't spoken since. We barely went more than a couple of days without talking. I was wrong, and I never got the chance to tell her that I was sorry. Oh God, why did you have to take my grandmother away? Why, Lord? I need my Granny! She's all I have left!" Shania said between sobs.

"She's not all you have left. You have your children, and you have us, your church family. Now, I want you to calm down and try to pull yourself together. It's going to be okay. Would you like us to pray with you?"

"What's the use? These last couple of years, I've been through more trials and pain than I've been through in my whole life. It seems like no matter how hard I try to do what's right, things keep going wrong. I think God is punishing me for something," Shania cried, feeling defeated.

"God is in not punishing you, Shania, nor has he forsaken you. Remember when I told you that when we make the choice to give our lives over to God, it can seem like any and everything that could go wrong will? It's the Devil's way of seeing if he can make us change our minds. We all go through this at some point," Tricia said.

"Yes, Sister Tricia is right," Jake said.

"That sounds like something that Granny would say," Shania said as she wiped her face.

"Your Granny was one wise lady. I'm glad we had the pleasure of meeting her. Her wisdom was invaluable," Jake commented.

"Come on in here, boys. Take hold of your mother's hand. We are going to pray together for your Granny's soul and for God to give this family the strength to get through this difficult time."

"God, our father. We pray for Sister Atkin's soul, which you take. So, she can take her place among your angels in heaven, Lord. We pray that you have mercy on her family here on earth. We ask that you be with them in their sorrow and in their time of need. If there were a time that they needed you, lord, it's now. We ask, through your son, Christ Jesus, that you give them the strength and grace they need to pull through and come out stronger on the other side. Have mercy on them, heavenly father, have mercy, in Jesus' name. We say amen."

After Jake prayed, he and Tricia left to tend to their other flock while Lydia stayed to make sure that the boys ate something. She tried to get Shania to eat something, too, but she said she didn't have an appetite. Trey called Zaria and told her the news about Granny.

"I can't thank you enough for being here, Lydia. Granny was my rock. At times like this, I could always count on her to pull me through. It's nice to know that I have you."

"It's my pleasure, Shania. You know I'm here for you all. Trey is going to take me home now, but I'll be back tomorrow. If you need anything, don't hesitate to give me a call," Lydia said as she hugged Shania and Zane.

The following afternoon, Gary picked up Shania's older sister, Cassandra, from the airport. When they arrived at Shania's house, Shania was surprised to see her get out of Gary's car alone without her family.

"Cass, I'm so glad to see you. Where're my nieces and nephew?"

"I didn't bring them. It's not like they were all that close to Granny."

"Cassandra, Granny practically raised us, and you didn't think it was important for them to attend her funeral?"

"They hardly knew her, Shania. Come on, give your big sis a hug. How are you, girl?"

"I'm trying to hang on," Shania replied.

"Well, I'm going to leave you two sisters alone so you can catch up on things," Gary said as he carried Cassandra's bags inside. "I still have a lot to do before the services."

I'm surprised that Granny didn't make all the arrangements herself before she passed," Cassandra said.

"As a matter of fact, she and I made most of her funeral arrangements over a year ago. I just got to make a few calls to finalize things," Gary replied.

"Why am I not surprised?" Cassandra said.

"Let us know what you need us to do, Uncle Gary," Shania said, purposely cutting her sister off.

"I'll come by sometime tomorrow so we can go over her obituary," he said before walking out the door.

Cassandra was a very attractive woman. She was very tall and had a slender body. She had shoulder-length chestnut brown hair that went well with her cinnamon skin tone. Her walk was graceful and cat-like. She looked like a model who owned the runway.

"This is a beautiful place you have here, sis." Cassandra said, "You guys did all right for yourselves."

"Yeah, Zach and I did okay." She said, her gaze aimed at the ground.

The house was on a hill that overlooked Stone Mountain. It was a two-story modern Tudor with a two-car garage that was converted into a family game room. The game room had a pool table, a dart game area, and a projector with a large screen and chairs so they could sit and watch movies. Zach had a carport built on the side of the house for their cars. Upstairs, there were four bedrooms and two full bathrooms. The master bedroom had its own suite. Downstairs was an eat-in kitchen with all modern appliances. Across from the kitchen was a large dining room. On the other side of the dining room was a large sunken family room. Next to the family room was a guest room with a full bathroom next to it. On the other side was a den that Zach used as his office.

"Cass, what happened between you and Granny that made you so angry with her?" Shania asked her as she prepared a light dinner.

"What makes you think I was angry with her?"

"You never came home to visit her, for one thing. The only time she got to see you or the kids was when they were born, and we came out there to see them and when we came out for Aunt Ruthie's funeral."

"I never felt comfortable around Granny. I had the feeling that she took us in because she had to. She didn't do it from her heart."

"Of course, she did it because she had to. Granny was practically finished raising her own kids, Cassy. You think she wanted to take on two more?"

"Yeah, well, she went out of her way to let us know that. So, I made things easy for her. When I left to go out west to college, I made up my mind that I wasn't coming back. You got anything that I can put in this ginger ale?" She asked as she held up a 20-ounce bottle of ale.

"You mean alcohol?"

"Yeah, I need something stronger than this. I had a long day. Don't tell me that you became so holy that you don't have anything to drink in the house."

"Yes, I do. Let me show you what I have." She said as she showed her their bar.

The next morning, Gary came over, and the three of them went over all the details pertaining to Granny's funeral, after which the three of them went to pick out her casket. The idea of choosing a coffin was too much for Shania. She couldn't handle it. After taking her home, Cassandra accompanied Gary to the funeral home to finalize the details of Granny's burial.

Granny's service was held at Ebenezer Baptist Church. People came from all over Georgia and other states to pay their respects. The church held a few hundred people, and every pew was filled. Granny had been a member there for more than 50 years, during the time when Martin Luther King Jr. was the Reverend. This was also where the Atlanta Tribune used to hold their secret meetings.

At the end of the services, Gary, Shania, and Cassandra greeted friends and family as they made their way to the coffin to pay their last respects before returning to their seats. A tall, dark, handsome, and impeccably dressed man walked up to the casket. They watched as he leaned over and kissed Granny on the forehead. He whispered a few words before touching her face affectionately. Shania and Cassandra both gasped as he turned and made his way towards them. Shania turned to Gary and said, "That's not …"

"Yes, that's your father."

"What's he doing here?" Cassandra, who was sitting on the other side of Gary, asked.

"He's paying his respects," Gary whispered under his breath as he stood up to greet him.

"Ray, it's good to see you," he said as he took both of Ray's hands into his.

"Good to see you too, Gary. It's been too long. Hello, girls," Ray said to them as he reached over to embrace them. Cassandra pulled back and handed him her hand. Noticing her aloofness, he settled for a handshake. He told them that he would see them at the burial.

"Why is he here?" Shania asked her uncle.

"Yeah, why? He never kept in touch with Granny all these years." Cassandra said.

"He's here to pay his respects just like everyone else who loved Granny. Besides, he did keep in touch with her. We'll talk about this later. Now's not the time." Gary said before greeting one of Granny's church members.

Once they were through greeting all the guests, it was the family's turn to pay their last respects. Shania and her kids made their way up to the coffin. Shania was determined to be strong and hold it together. Even though every inch of her body wanted to jump in and lay beside her grandmother like she used to do when she was a girl. She managed to hold her composure while up at the coffin. She said a few words to Granny and asked for her forgiveness before kissing her on her cheeks.

To everyone's surprise, it was Cassandra who broke down. At first, she didn't want to go to the coffin to pay her last respects. But after some coaxing from Gary, she allowed him to escort her. She took one look at her grandmother and fell apart. The last time she saw Granny was ten years ago at her Aunt Ruth Anne's funeral. Granny was still spry and full of life then. She didn't expect to see this small, frail, lifeless woman, who barely took up half the coffin lying there. It was all too much for her. The guilt she felt from disassociating herself from her and the pain of another major loss overtook her. She nearly collapsed onto the floor before Gary and Trey caught her and broke her fall. They took her back to her seat and sat with her until she was able to recompose herself.

Outside, the sky opened up and began pouring down as everyone ran to their cars and headed to the burial. A half-hour later, as they made their way across the cemetery to Granny's final resting place, the pastor said that even the Angels were crying for Granny, except they were crying with joy instead of sorrow. He said that even though everyone will miss her, the angels needed her in heaven more than we did down here. At her gravesite, he said a few final words and a prayer. The service ended with the choir singing Granny's favorite song, "Take Me Home," which brought everyone present to tears, including Gary.

Just as all the guests began walking to their cars, a bolt of lightning lit up the heavens and flashed across the sky. Seconds later came a loud roar. Pastor Jones laughed and said, "That's our Sister Atkins having the last word." The crowd roared with laughter and burst into a round of applause.

During the ride back to the church for the farewell dinner, Gary decided that this was a good time to talk to Shania and Cassandra about their father. First, he talked about how well the service went. Then he said, "I want to give you all a heads-up. Your father is going to meet us back at the Church to have dinner with us and catch up on things. I hope you two will give him a better reception than you did during the service."

"Why is he showing up all of a sudden after all these years? What's up with that?" Shania asked.

"Yeah, after he just up and left us, he has the nerve to show up at Granny's funeral?" Cassandra said.

"Don't judge him before you know the whole story," Gary said.

"All I know is that no one's seen him since Mama died. So why is he here now?" Cassy asked angrily.

"He has the right to come and pay his respects like everyone else," Gary replied.

"No, he doesn't, not after what he put Granny through," Cassy answered.

"What did he put her through, Cassy?" He asked.

"First, he abandoned us. Then, he left us with Granny to raise us alone. He could have come back for us after our mother died, but he left us with Granny without any money or anything. We haven't heard as much as a peep from him," Cassy said.

"You don't have a clue about what happened back then."

"Well, enlighten us, Uncle Gary, please," Cassy snapped.

"First of all, he didn't abandon you all. Your mother asked him to leave."

"Why would she ask him to leave his family? He must have done something for her to tell him to leave," Cassy answered.

"Ray is one of the kindest people I know. You girls meant the world to him, and he would have never left you on his own. Your mother had breast cancer. When she first found out, she made him promise not to tell anyone. Then she asked him to leave because she did not want him to watch her die and feel sorry for her. She said she wanted him to remember her the way she was. Sandra was a vain woman; may she rest in peace. Your father refused to leave. He wanted her to fight the cancer. He told Mama about her cancer, hoping she would intervene. Your mother became furious with him and threw him out. Sandy was really stubborn like that. Once she had her mind made up about something, nothing could change it. She got that from Mama, I suppose. Ray was and is a good man. He made sure you girls were taken care of. He sent Mama a check the first week of every month until you girls were grown."

124

"If he was so good, why didn't he ever come to see us? Better yet, why didn't he take us with him after our mama died?" Cassandra asked.

"Because he was consumed with grief; after she died, he nearly fell apart. He knew she had cancer, but he didn't expect it to take her so soon. I believe she died quickly because she was grieving, too. She knew she'd made the wrong decision, but she wouldn't go back on it. The grief ate her up inside just as quickly as the cancer did."

"Granny never said one word. She just acted like we were a burden on her. And here she was getting money from our dad all along." Cassandra said.

"Money wasn't the issue, Cassy. Mama was grieving herself. You've got to remember she had just lost a child. As a matter of fact, she lost two children. I don't know if you remember, but just months before your mother died, my brother JJ died unexpectedly. He was walking across the railroad tracks one night and got run over by a train. They believed he was drunk at the time. He was only 24 years old. It hit Mama hard. Before she could get over the death of one child, she lost another one."

"I remember Uncle JJ. Granny kept his picture on her dresser. I remember asking her about him. All she would say is that he went to be with the Lord. I never understood what she meant by that until I got older," Shania said.

"I remember the day they buried him." Cassandra said, "Mama wouldn't let us go to the funeral. She made us go to school that day. Uncle JJ was my favorite. No offense, Uncle Gary."

"None taken," he replied, smiling.

"I remember for a long time after Mama died, Granny would play Brook Benton's song 'Rainy Night in Georgia.' She played that song over and over again," Shaina recalled.

"Sure did. I guess that was her way of grieving," Gary said. "After Sandy died, mama had to take you girls in before she had a chance to grieve properly for JJ. Taking care of you girls is what she needed. It kept her busy and kept her mind off her sorrows. I believe that's what got her through those times. Both she and Ray did the best they could, given the circumstances. Ray adored your Granny as much as he adored your mother. He wouldn't have missed her funeral for anything in the world. So please, honor her today and be nice to him."

"We will, Uncle Gary," Shania answered remorsefully.

As the three of them entered the church, they heard the choir singing "Jesus Loves Me." The aroma of the different foods met them at the door.

"I wasn't hungry before, but I sure am now that I smell all this good food," Cassandra said.

"Mama used to say, 'There's nothing better than church folks' cooking," Gary replied as they made their way down the stairs to the basement where the meal was being served.

"Amen," Shania said somberly.

Brother Fulton was standing at the bottom of the stairs, greeting people as they arrived. "All right, the family's all here," he yelled to someone behind him. "We saved you all a table up front."

"Brother Fulton, are those your yeast rolls I smelled as soon as we walked through the door?" Gary asked.

"You know they are," Brother Fulton responded, "I know how your mama loved my rolls. I couldn't send her off without them. Praise God," he answered with a wide grin. "You all go in and make yourselves comfortable. Sister Betty will be over to see what you'd like to eat," he said.

"Everything smells delicious, Brother Fulton. I know you all knocked yourselves out," Shania said.

Well, you know how we do here at Ebenezer. If your grandma was here, she would be throwing down with us. Sister Betty said just this morning, the only thing missing from the dessert table was Sister Juanita's bread pudding and her special banana sauce," he said with a smile.

Cassandra couldn't believe her eyes when she saw all the food the church had set up on two large tables. There was roasted turkey, glazed ham with pineapple, fried chicken, roast beef, roast pork, barbecue ribs, blackened catfish, cabbage, mixed greens, glazed carrots, string beans, a green toss salad, seafood salad, potato salad, red beans and rice, macaroni and cheese, and vegetable lasagna. Right across from the food tables was one long table with two rows of every kind of homemade dessert imaginable. There was a variety of cakes, including chocolate, coconut, lemon coconut, Pineapple upside down, red velvet, carrot cake, and banana pudding. There was also an assortment of homemade pies, including apple, sweet potato, cherry, coconut custard, lemon meringue, and Sister Betty's famous peach cobbler. There were different kinds of breads, but nothing smelled better than Brother Fulton's fresh yeast rolls.

"Oh Lord, now this is a feast fit for a queen," Cassandra said.

Ray stood up as Gary, Cassandra, and Shania reached their table. He held out the chairs for each of them to sit.

"Boy, that was some send-off, wasn't it?" he commented. Shania and Cassandra both nodded their heads in agreement.

"I sure hope you all are good and hungry because there's enough food here to feed an army," he said after everyone was seated." Church folks sure know how to burn."

"Yes, Lord," Gary answered.

"I remember the after-church dinners Granny used to make every Sunday. If you didn't make it to church that Sunday, she wouldn't let you have any dessert," Ray continued.

"That was Mama," Gary said.

"You remember that, Ray?" Cassandra asked, surprised that he remembered.

"I sure do," he laughed, "Granny would say if you can't partake of the Lord's food, then you can't partake of any treats." They all laughed, remembering Granny and her rules.

Just then, Betty Fulton walked up to the front of the dining room and asked that everyone settle down so that the Reverend could bless the food. Afterward, she escorted the family up to the food table so that they could get their plates before the others.

"Now, if there's anything else you all want, come on up to the front; don't stand in line. This dinner is for the family; everyone else here is a guest," Sister Betty said.

"Thank you, Sister Betty," Shania said.

"Sister Juanita would have done the same thing for me if she was here. Lord, what am I going to do without my buddy?" she said as she walked away, wiping the tears from her eyes with the bottom of her apron.

Gary's talk helped make Ray's reunion with Shania and Cassandra go smoothly. Although they were still apprehensive about him and did not understand why he never tried to be a part of their lives, they no longer felt bitter or resentful towards him. Shania proudly introduced him to her children, who sat across from them at the table. Cassandra showed Ray pictures of her three kids. Cassandra, who favored him herself, wanted Ray to see how much her son Ricky looked like him. For the rest of the evening, Shania and Cassandra competed for Ray's attention. They tried to keep the conversation on the present, careful not to bring up the past.

"Shania, I heard that you lost your husband recently," Ray said.

"Yeah, it's going on two years since we lost Zach," Shania answered sadly.

"That must have been terrible for you all. I'm sorry for not being there for you during that time."   `

"Thanks. I appreciate your concern. I know one thing; I wouldn't have made it through if it weren't for Granny. Lord knows that woman was my rock."

"Granny was everyone's rock. She always had been. She was a strong woman. Everyone here has nothing but good things to say about her," Ray replied.

"Yes. She was loved by her church family, for sure," Shania answered sadly.

"You don't find many women who have been through all she has and was still willing to help others the way she did," Ray said.

"Granny always said that doing something for others helps distract you from your own troubles."

"You must have followed Granny's advice, Shania because it seems like you and your kids are holding up pretty well."

"It's been hard on us. We're still adjusting to the change. But with the grace of God, we're pulling through."

"Well, my husband Richard's been gone for several years now, and my kids and I made out just fine without anyone," Cassandra said bitterly.

"You lost your husband too, Cassandra?" Ray asked, surprised to hear it. He and Granny had spoken on occasion, and he didn't remember her ever mentioning it.

"Not in the way Shania did. We're divorced. I'm surprised the son of a gun agreed to take the kids this week so that I could come home for Granny's funeral. I give it two days before he drops them off at his sister's house."

"I didn't know that you and Richard were divorced," Shania said as she turned to Gary. "Did you know that Uncle Gary?"

"Nope. This is the first I've heard of it."

"That's because I didn't tell anyone, not even Granny. I didn't want to burden you all with my problems. I threw his sorry butt out several years ago."

"I can't believe you never said anything to us all these years," Shania said.

"I did, but no one was listening."

"Well, we're listening now," Ray said as he put his hand on hers. "If there's anything I can do for you or my grandkids, Cassandra, let me know. Even if you just want to talk. That goes for you, too, Shania."

They both nodded.

"There sure are enough of them, Huh Ray?" Gary said, laughing.

"Yes, and they're all beautiful too," Ray said, looking over at Shania's kids sitting across the table, his chest stuck out like a proud Grandpa.

"God, don't they have anything stronger than pop or this weak-ass punch?" Cassandra barked.

"That was uncalled for, Cassandra," Gary said, annoyed.

"I'm just saying, Uncle Gary, even Jesus served wine to his guest." She was clearly sipping on something other than pop.

Shania and Gary looked at each other. Neither said a word. They both knew this was Cassandra's way of getting attention. Besides, when she thought no one was looking, they saw her pour something from a flask that she took out of her purse into her cup under the table.

Growing up, Cassandra was always a Daddy's girl. She was 44 years old and was still a spitting image of Ray. She's tall and lanky like him and has his rich cinnamon complexion as well as his long, narrow face. Everyone knew that she was the apple of her father's eye. She was eleven years old when Ray moved out and just turned twelve when their mother died. Cassandra had fond memories of the times she spent with Ray. She cherished those times. She never got over his leaving.

Shania, on the other hand, just turned 40. She looked more like her mother and Granny than Ray. She's on the shorter side with a petite figure. She also has a full, round face and her mama's and granny's golden honey complexion. She was eight years old when her life suddenly took a turn. She had a difficult time adapting to the changes, especially her mother's death. Granny became her lifeboat, and Shania clung to her from that day on.

Ray, Cassandra, and Shania spent the next few days catching up on each other's lives in Shania's family room. Ray shared stories about their childhood with them. Most of which Cassandra remembered. What Shania remembered most was when her mother took ill.

Ray told them about his travels and how he lived in different states before settling back in Atlanta and opening a car dealership. Cassandra was surprised to hear that he lived out west, only a few hours from where she lived.

"Did you at least think about us, Ray?" Cassandra asked, longing to know.

"There wasn't a day that went by when I didn't think about you girls."

"Why did you leave us?"

"Things were complicated back then, Cassandra."

"Aren't they always?"

"I see you're not going to make this easy."

"Why didn't you come back for us after Mama died?"

"After your mother died, I fell apart. It was as though she took a part of me with her. I was so messed up. I didn't think I could take care of you girls. Cassandra, you were twelve. You were on your way to becoming a young lady. I didn't think I was able to take care of you the way you needed me to."

"But Ray, you were all we had left."

"We had Granny too, Cassy," replied Shania, feeling the need to come to his defense. Cassandra glared her eyes at Shania.

"I was so heartbroken at the time I couldn't even think straight," Ray continued. "I knew I wouldn't be able to give you girls the stability you needed. I kept thinking if only I'd stayed, maybe I could have taken care of her, maybe she could have survived. Your grandmother told me to stay and fight for her and with her. I wanted to, but your mother wouldn't let me. When your mother found out that she had cancer, she insisted that I leave; she said she didn't want me to see her wasting away into nothing. I told her that none of that mattered; I was there for better or worse. I told her that we would get through this together. She said she wasn't going to allow me to watch her wither away and die. I didn't know where to turn, so I went to your grandmother. I was hoping she'd be able to talk some sense into her. But she became furious that I went to her mother, and she told me to get out. When I refused to leave, she started throwing my clothes out the window and threatened to call the police if I didn't leave, so I did. I know your Granny thought I was a coward for not staying, but I didn't see a choice."

"Granny was strong-willed, but she was pretty good at reading people," Shania said.

"She always said we were a family of strong-willed women. She was right," Cassandra said to Shania before turning back to her father.

"Why didn't you at least visit us?" She asked Ray." You just disappeared like we didn't exist. All we needed was you, Daddy. Especially since our mama was gone," she said in a sad, childlike voice.

"I know, baby, and I'm so sorry that I didn't come to see you. I'm here now, and I'm here to stay."

The night before Cassandra left, she came to the family with a bottle of Harvey's Bristol Cream and a bottle of Johnny Walker Red. Shania walked in from the kitchen and saw Cassy holding up two bottles.

"Shania, do you still drink Harvey's Bristol Cream?" she called out to her as she sat the bottles on the table in the family room.

"To tell you the truth, I rarely drink anything, maybe a glass of wine here and there. Girl, I can't even remember the last time I had Harvey's Bristol," Shania answered.

"Well, after these last few days, I need a drink. I should have asked you to bring two glasses with ice while you were in the kitchen." Cassandra said.

"I'll get them now," she said as they walked back into the kitchen. She needs a drink, really? Shania thought to herself. That's all she's been doing since she got here. She isn't fooling anyone but herself. She braced herself before going back into the living room with the glasses.

"Shania, this is a nice music system you have here. What is it, Bose? Put on some music, girl."

"What do you want to hear?"

"I want to hear something nice and smooth. Here, pour yourself a drink," she said as she handed her the bottle of Bristol Cream. "We should call Ray to come over." It was obvious that she had already begun.

"I just spoke to Dad a few minutes ago. He said he was going to go to the garage. He wanted to check in and make sure everything was okay. He said he was going to be there for a couple of hours." Shania replied as she put on an old Alexander Hamilton CD.

"Do you think he really owns that car dealership?"

"Of course I do. I don't think he would lie about something like that."

"What do we really know about him? For all we know, he could be telling us anything, and we wouldn't know the difference."

"If that's the case, why say anything at all?"

"All I'm saying is that we don't know Ray that well. We gotta be careful. Can't believe everything people tell us."

"People? He's our father, Cassy. Don't you think it's disrespectful to call him Ray? What would Granny say if she heard you call Dad by his first name?"

"Well, Granny isn't here now, is she?" After seeing the expression on her sister's face, Cassandra laughed and said, "Oh, come on. Lighten up, will you? I'm just playing. Tell me, how are you really holding up, sis? And I don't want to hear all that crap you've been feeding Ray. Oh, sorry, I mean Dad; I forgot how sensitive you can be."

"Zach's death was hard, especially in the beginning. I wished he would have just walked out on us instead of killing himself. At least I could have cursed him out and let him know how I felt and be done. Now I can't even tell him how selfish he was for leaving us," Shania said.

"You don't wish he would have just walked out. It's not that simple. Remember when I said that I threw Richard out? Truth be told, he left me. Believe me; there were times when I wished he was dead. At least it would have been over, and I would have had closure. The way things are now, I still got to deal with his sorry ass because of the kids. I know that sounds awful, but the truth is, both situations are messed up. Sometimes, we think the grass is greener on the other side when, in truth, it's just as bad. What we have to do is get over it. The problem is that I don't know how."

"Well, drinking's not the way."

"But it sure helps," Cassandra laughed as she poured herself another drink.

"Turning to God is what helped me. I can't say that I'm there yet, but I'm sure in a better place than I was a year and a half ago. I tell you one thing: if I had a chance to do things all over again, I would follow God's word and do things his way."

"Do you think that would have made a difference, Shania? Zach was messed up way before you married him; I don't think doing things God's way would have changed that."

"I said I would have done things God's way. I can't speak for Zach. If I had practiced the fruits of the spirit, you know, like love, kindness, and patience? It may have helped Zach."

"I doubt it. From what I saw, you were always patient. I remember Zach was weak. Even as a kid, he was weak."

"He wasn't weak; he just wasn't good at making decisions. He was very easygoing and kind; I mistook his kindness for weakness. Not that I meant to. I saw it as my way of getting things done. Granny used to say 'someone has to take the lead.'

"And, you think that's why he killed himself? If that was the case, he would have done that a long time ago. It had to be something deeper than that," Cassy, the therapist, replied.

"Yeah, I'm sure it was."

"You didn't see any signs?"

"I did, but I was afraid to address it, so I ignored them. He had become so withdrawn that last year. Suddenly, he just distanced himself from us, as if he didn't want anything to do with us. He wouldn't go on any family outings. He wouldn't eat dinner at the table with us anymore, even on the holidays. He became so secretive like he was hiding something. He even stopped having sex with me. It'd been years since we were intimate."

"Do you think he was having an affair?"

"I don't think he was having an affair because, after work, he was always home. He just lost interest in the family. In handling the finances, everything."

"Wow, that's deep."

"Yeah," Shania said as she poured herself another glass of Harvey's. "What made it so bad was that the more I took control of things, the more he withdrew. I don't know why he took his own life, Cass."

"Men are selfish, Shania. Zach, of all people, knew the effect that this would have on you all. He knew how devastated he was when his father took his own life. He knew that you and those kids were depending on him, and he knew what this would do to you. Not to speak ill of the dead, but he just didn't care.

"Zach wasn't selfish by nature, Cassy. I believe he may have known, but I don't think he could have helped it. I think it was out of his control. Someone told me that hurting people hurt people."

"Well, I'm glad you and the kids reached out for help. It seemed like it worked. I'm sorry I didn't come up for his funeral. I had so much going on that I didn't think I would have been any comfort to you."

"I understand, but a phone call from my big sister would have been nice," Shania replied, not really understanding. Men are not the only selfish ones, she thought to herself.

"I'm sorry, but I didn't know what to say. You did get the flowers I sent, didn't you?"

"Yes, we did. They were lovely. So, tell me about you and Richard," she inquired.

"Well, you know Richard and I met in college. At the time, he had been dating someone else for about two years, and he broke up with her for me, so I thought. During my senior year, when I became pregnant with LaShawn, I found out that she was also pregnant by him. He claimed that it was over between them, so I made him marry me to prove it. Granny always said the way you start out is the way you'll end up. She was right because Richard ran around with other women our entire marriage, and I accepted it for a while. I finally got tired and began to cheat, too. Since I accepted his cheating, I expected him to accept mine. But when he found out, he couldn't handle it. He told me I was a better person than he was, and he bailed out."

"What did you expect, Cassy?"

"I knew better than to expect anything different from him. All I'm saying is that the signs were there from the beginning, just like the signs were there with Zach. Zach was always strange when you met in high school. You know that yourself."

"I know, but I thought I could help him."

"The only person who could have helped him was a psychiatrist, and even that wasn't a guarantee."

"You're right."

"I know you're in pain, and now you have to deal with Granny's death. We both do, but believe me, it'll get better," Cassandra said.

"I hope so. I know one thing: I'll never judge an alcoholic or drug addict again. I really understand how they can turn to something to ease their emotional pain," Shania said.

"I'll drink to that," Cassy said as she sipped from her glass.

"I have a new respect for them. Life can be so cruel, and sometimes people can't handle the stress. They need something to ease their pain."

"I'll drink to that too," taking another sip from her glass.

"I'm being serious, Cass. Life is not a joke."

"I'm serious, too. Why do you think I drink like this? Just to feel good. I drink so I can get through each miserable day."

"I'm sorry. I didn't realize until you got here how much pain you are in."

"How could you have known? I'm not one to wear my feelings on my sleeve."

"Did you ever think about going for help? You know, to find out what the source of your pain is?"

"Oh, I know what the source of my pain is. I'm a therapist, remember? I do what I got to do."

"What about your kids? Don't you think this is affecting them?"

"Look, Shania, my kids are doing fine, okay? I don't want to talk about this anymore; let it go."

"Okay," Shania answered reluctantly.

"I thought I could've saved Zach from himself when, in reality, there wasn't anything I could do. Taking on that kind of responsibility can be a heavy load. We place a huge burden on ourselves when we think we can save someone. I believe that was the case with me and Zach. If there were anything I learned since his death, it's that only God can change people."

"You're right. That's why you can't blame yourself for his actions," Cassandra said.

"I keep thinking if only I knew why he killed himself," she whispered.

"Would knowing why he killed himself really make a difference? It won't change things, you know."

"I know it won't. But at least I'll have some closure."

"I've learned that some things we are better off not knowing."

"And I've learned that trying to repay a person for hurting us never works," Shania replied, trying to shift the conversation. "We have to leave that up to God. When we try to repay them on our own, it can backfire, which I believe was the case with Richard."

He deserved it," Cassandra snapped.

"Maybe he did, but it's up to God to handle him. He's not going to allow people to do wrong for so long. We don't have to take matters into our own hands. God has a way of shutting people down. He will stop them in their tracks when they least expect it."

"Do you really believe that Shania?"

"Yes, I do. I saw what he has done to people who've done wrong, and I saw what he has done for those who believe."

Ray had moved out at a vulnerable time for the family, particularly for Cassandra, who was just entering adolescence. Because of his leaving, Cassandra developed a fear that she could never be loved. From the time he left, it seemed like she was on a quest to relive the pain of his leaving over and over again.

During high school, Cassandra began dating boys who were in a relationship with someone else. She carried this behavior into her college days. Her need to be loved was so deep that she believed that if a man left his significant other for her, that meant he really loved her. If he refused to leave his relationship, then she would get rid of him, only to repeat the vicious cycle all over again.

"The mood in here is too depressing. Play something a little more upbeat," Cassandra asked.

"The kids have all the latest music upstairs. All I have down here are the oldies but goodies. Oh, do you want to hear something by Beyonce?" she said as she held up one of her CD's before putting it in the CD player.

"Yeah, that's what I'm talking about. Come on; let's dance," Cassandra said.

Just then, Zaria walked into the living room to see what was going on. She stood there, watching her mother and aunt dance. Before long, Cassandra grabbed her arm and said, "Come on, Zaria, dance with us."

Zaria joined in and started dancing with both her mother and her aunt. A few minutes later, Trey and Zane heard the music from the kitchen. They stood in the entryway to the family room as they watched the girls dance. When Cassandra saw them, she took their hands and tried to pull them into the family room to join in. They both declined.

"Look at mom," Zane said when Cassandra went back to her dancing. "She had a few drinks, and now, she's acting crazy."

"What's wrong with her having a little fun? When's the last time you saw her laughing and enjoying herself?" Trey said in her defense.

"When's the last time you saw her drinking? Never," Zane said as he walked away.

Shania heard them, but she kept dancing and pretended that she didn't hear anything. Early the next morning, Ray picked Cassandra up and took her to the airport.

Chapter Six

Ray

After Sandra died, Ray moved around the country for a few years. He lived in New York City, California, Las Vegas and Virginia before settling back in Atlanta, where he opened a used car dealership. He remarried for a short time when he lived in Las Vegas but didn't have any more children.

He adored his grandsons, and he enjoyed spending time with them. Ray and Trey gravitated towards each other, and they immediately created a special bond. Ray had such a calm and laid-back personality that Trey became fond of him. Although Zach also had a laid-back personality, he never made any real effort to bond with any of his kids. Therefore, Trey never felt close to him.

Ray, on the other hand, shared stories about his family's history with Trey and Zane, which intrigued them. Trey loved hearing about his family's history, especially since neither Shania nor Zach talked much about their families. Every once in a while, when Granny was in a talkative mood, she would tell him stories about her family. Then, as quickly as she began telling them about her life, she would stop. They could see that the pain from her losses was too much for her.

Ray opened a new awakening in the boys. He took them fishing and camping. He attended Zane's baseball games at the church. He even drove the whole family to Zaria's school in Tuskegee for family day.

Even though his relationship with his family was going well, Ray's used car dealership wasn't. The younger generation wasn't in the market for used cars. They didn't want their first cars to be old hoopties the way his generation did. They wanted to drive new and expensive SUV's and luxury cars. When Ray learned that Trey had a bachelor's degree in business management, he offered him a job at his dealership, hoping that he would bring in some young, fresh ideas to help improve his business. He had always wished he had someone who was able to take over his business when he retired. Trey was excited to learn about the business and to be working full-time with his grandpa.

Ray came from a long line of entrepreneurs. His father sold insurance from door to door before opening one of Atlanta's first black life insurance companies. His grandfather was a blacksmith who also owned his own business. He had a witty personality and prided himself on his honesty. His grandfather was so trustworthy that people reportedly brought their horses all the way from New Orleans so he could shoe them. His father, Ray Sr., was a hard man.

Ray and Sandra met at a college dance. Ray was a Junior at the prestigious Morehouse College in Atlanta, and Sandra was a sophomore at Morehouse's sister school, Spelman College. Ray dated a lot of Spelman girls, but he felt that most of them were phony and superficial. Sandra, on the other hand, was real. She spoke up for what she believed in and stood by those beliefs even when no one else did. Ray and Sandra dated for a year before he asked her to marry him.

Ray's father, Raymond Sr., was against their marriage from the start, not because he didn't like Sandra. She had the right complexion

146

and attended the right school. He didn't want Ray to marry Sandra because of her mother. He knew Juanita for many years and thought she was a smart, fine, upright woman when she was married to Jackson Atkins. After Jackson was killed, Juanita tried to stay home to raise her family, but with four children to feed and clothe, she was forced to take on odd jobs here and there to support her family. That's when Ray's father and other prominent black men in Atlanta began to distance themselves from her.

Even though Juanita had excellent writing skills due to the editing work she'd done while working at the paper, other negro newspapers were afraid to hire her after Jackson's death. So, on occasion, when things became difficult for her financially, she would go out to the deep waters to catch and sell fish and other seafood out of the back of her car to support her family. She also sold fried fish dinners on Fridays, chopped and sold wood, and whatever else she could do to feed her four children.

Ray Sr. and some of the other men from her church thought that she was too unconventional for a woman at the time. They thought she would be better off if she found a man and got remarried. Juanita knew that her chances of finding a husband who was willing to take on a two-time widow with four children were slim to none. She wanted all her children to get a proper education. She learned from her father that the only way to do this was through hard work. It wasn't until the latter part of the Korean War that she was able to secure a steady job in a factory, sewing collars on uniforms for the servicemen. This was when her family's finances began to improve. In the end, she was able to set the example for her family that hard work paid off.

Ray Sr. had his own issues. He hated anyone with dark skin, including himself and his sons. He made it his mission to marry a light-skinned woman in the hopes of having light-skinned children. His two sons, Ray Jr. and Reggie, were dark like him. His daughter, Raynell, had a light complexion like her mother. Although he worshiped the ground his daughter walked on, he despised his wife for being everything he was not. He would beat her and his sons every chance he got because of his own insecurities.

Sandra was the opposite of Ray Jr. in many ways. But instead of resenting her the way his father had resented his mother, he admired her for it. She was confident, gregarious, outgoing, and loved life. She liked to have a good time. At the same time, she knew how to take care of business. Ray was intelligent but shy and serious by nature. He was not as comfortable with the party scene as Sandra was, but for her, he pretended he was.

When they met at Morehouse, Ray was living on campus. He not only wanted to get away from his father, but he also wanted to experience dorm life. Sandra was a part-time student at Spelman College and lived at home instead of on campus. She knew that her mother wanted her and her siblings to go to college full-time, but she also knew that they were struggling after her older sister, Ruth Anne, left to go out west to attend the University of California. Sandra worked part-time while attending college to help pay for her expenses.

Ray fell madly in love with Sandra and was determined to marry her, even though he knew his father had issues with strong, independent women like Sandra and her mother. He, on the other hand, had problems with passive women, like his mother, who allowed his father to beat her and her sons. He was determined to be everything his father was not. He wanted to show him that he was a kind and respected businessman like his grandfather.

Sandra, like many women at the time, did not complete college; instead, she chose to get married and have children. Juanita was not too happy with her decision. Ruth Anne went on to finish college and became a high school biology teacher, eventually becoming the first black female Vice Principal in the Oakland, California school system.

Juanita knew there was no way that Sandra would reconsider her decision to get married. Sandra was as determined and as stubborn as she was at her age, and this worried her even more.

Ray, who was Sandra's senior by two years, graduated a month before he and Sandra got married. Ray Sr. refused to help with any of the wedding expenses because he felt that it was the bride's responsibility. Everyone from Juanita's church pitched in to help with the wedding. Some prepared food; others donated the flowers and decorations. One sister from her church made the dresses for the maid of honor and bridesmaids. Sandra was able to save money from her part-time job to buy the wedding gown of her dreams. A close friend of Juanita's, who owned several acres of land, allowed them to have their reception on her lawn. Ray's brother, Reggie, was their photographer.

Ray and Sandra had a beautiful but modest garden wedding. It wasn't the society wedding that Ray's sister had, but it was a spectacular affair attended by many.

Ray worked at his father's insurance company. Even though he had a degree in business, his father made him start at the bottom as a door-to-door insurance agent. He wasn't making much money at the time. Sandra thought this was unfair, and she expressed this to Ray Sr., which made him dislike her even more.

Ray was very happy with Sandra, but he couldn't have been happier when their first child, Cassandra, was born and four years later when Sandra gave birth to their second daughter, Shania. Ray worked hard to support his family, and he made sure to be there for them when he was not working. Every Sunday after church, the whole family would get together at Granny's for dinner. He and the kids adored Granny. Things were picture-perfect until Sandra suddenly became ill.

Chapter Seven
The Family Business

A few weeks after Granny's funeral, Noel Fulton, Granny's lawyer, called the family together for the reading of her will. Cassandra was unable to attend, so she asked Noel to send her a transcript of the reading. When she learned that Granny had left most of the few assets she had for Gary, she became irate and called Shania to let her know what she thought.

"Shania, can you believe that Granny left everything to Uncle Gary?" Cassandra said, clearly upset.

"Of course I can. She left what little she had to her only living child. I would have done the same thing; besides, she didn't leave everything to him." Shania answered.

"She left him her insurance policies, her house, her money in the bank, everything. That's not right. What about us or our children? Don't we deserve something?"

"Uncle Gary did practically everything for Granny. He worked hard to make sure she had everything she needed. He never married nor had any children of his own. He sacrificed his whole life for her."

"No one told him not to get married. That was his choice."

"And it was Granny's choice to leave everything to him. Come on, Cassy, you know Granny worked menial jobs for most of her life.

When she got sick and had to stop working, her social security wasn't enough for her to live on. Uncle Gary had to sell his house and move in with her so she could live comfortably. She didn't have anything to leave him but her house, which is almost a hundred years old and has more problems than it's worth."

"She left him her insurance policies and her bank account."

"What are you talking about? Those old policies weren't even enough to pay her burial expenses. And as for the money in the bank, they had a joint account. For all we know, most of that money could've been his."

"I just feel like she could have left us something."

"She did leave us something. She left me all the family pictures, her bibles, and a few other odds and ends. She left you mama's wedding rings, her best jewelry, and a fur coat. Shoot, you made out better than I did".

"What do I want with Mama's old wedding rings? I don't even wear my own wedding rings. And what am I going to do with a fur coat in Cali? Was Granny even thinking about me?"

"What is wrong with you, Cassandra? Those rings are a family heirloom. They have a history. And she left you her fur coat because you always raved about it. How do you have the nerve to be so ungrateful when you never even made an attempt to come and visit her once since you left home over twenty years ago?"

"I may not have visited her, but I kept in touch with her. I sent her cards and gifts."

"Yeah, you called her once a year on her birthday, and you sent her a card and flowers for Mother's Day. Shucks, you're lucky she left you anything. If you don't want the rings, at least pass them on to your girls. Better yet, give them to me. I'll make sure they stay in the family."

"I think I'll give them to Ray. He would love to have something from Mama."

"Cassy, I don't know what happened to you that made you so bitter, but I know it has to be more than you being uncomfortable around Granny."

"I don't mean to be bitter. I had a bad marriage.'

"Who hasn't? You need to work on learning how to forgive, let go of your resentment, and move on with your life. I'm going to pray for you."

"Oh, so, now that you're going to church, you think you've got to pray for me? Well, you can save the theatrics; I'm not buying it. I know the real you, Shania. You're pretty selfish yourself, missy. Don't think that I don't know how you treated Zach. You had him wrapped around your little fingers all those years. That's how you got that big ol' house sitting up on the hill and that fancy car of yours."

Shania was so shocked at what she was hearing that she could not respond. She knew her sister had some serious issues, but she didn't know how deep they were.

"And what's this I hear about Ray giving Trey a job at his car dealership?" Cassandra continued.

"Just that. Dad hired Trey to work with him since Trey has a degree in business management."

"What does selling cars have to do with business management?"

"Selling cars is a business, Cassandra; besides, Trey has to start somewhere."

"You're probably the one who put him up to hiring Trey. I bet you're just trying to get in good with Ray so he could leave Trey his business."

"What are you talking about, Cassandra?"

"It's no secret that you were both mama's and Granny's favorite. Why do you think I left and never came back?" Cassy asked, not waiting for an answer.

"You think I didn't notice how mama fussed over you until the day she died? Then Granny took over, cuddling you just like mama did. After Ray left, I never stood a chance. I tell you one thing; I'll be damned if my kids and I are going to be left out of his will too."

Shania never realized until after Granny died how much of an effect Ray's leaving had on her big sister. "You got some real serious issues. Look, I can't talk to you anymore. I gotta go," she said before she hung up.

Now I know what Granny must have felt after talking to me. Lord, I hope I wasn't that bad, Shania thought. Her thoughts went back to the last conversation she had with Granny, and she felt terrible about blaming her for not talking Trey out of going into the Air Force. She asked God to forgive her for the way she treated Granny.

Shania tried going back to work right after Granny's death but found that she wasn't able to focus on the job. Tricia suggested that she take some time off to get herself together. She assured her that her job would still be there.

Shania went into a tailspin. She began drinking a lot more and eventually began to neglect her responsibilities around the house. She knew it was time for her to get back to work.

Chapter Eight
Things Can't Get Any Worse, Can They?

A few months after Granny's funeral, Zaria came home for spring break. All she did was mope around the house for the entire break as if she'd lost her best friend. Shania knew that the last few years had been hard on her. She figured that she was either still trying to adjust to the loss of her father and Granny, or she was having separation issues with her boyfriend, Chad. She and Chad had been dating for a year, and Shania worried that they were moving too fast. She planned to have a one-on-one talk with her before Zaria went back to Alabama.

The next morning, Zaria came into the kitchen looking like something the cat dragged in.

"Zaria, why don't you take a shower and get dressed so we can go out for breakfast, just the two of us? We haven't had a girl's day out in a while," Shania suggested.

"No thanks, Mom. I'm not hungry. I'm just going to have a glass of OJ," She replied.

"All you're having is a glass of orange juice. Girl, the way you always carry on about how important it is to eat breakfast. What's wrong with you? Are you sick?" Shania asked, feeling her forehead.

"No, Mom, I just have a lot on my mind."

"Oh yeah, like what? Want to talk about it?"

"No, Mom."

"Is it Chad? Did you two break up?"

"I don't want to talk about it," she said before dragging herself slowly up the stairs.

"Well, I'm here if you need to talk," Shania called after her.

Spring break ended, and Zaria went back to school. Shania never did get the chance to find out what was bothering her. She was a little concerned, but she trusted that she raised her children to know that they could come to her whenever they had a problem, regardless of what it was.

Two weeks later, Shania was in the kitchen, fixing dinner for her and the boys, when the front doorbell rang. This was unusual because most people who came by called before coming and entered through the carport on the side of the house. When she looked out of the window, she was surprised to see Zaria and Chad standing there with their bags. She also noticed a taxi pulling out of the driveway.

"What in the world?" she said as she opened the front door. "Why didn't you call to let us know you were coming home, Zaria? Someone would have picked you up at the station."

"I wanted to surprise you."

"You did a good job of that. Hi, Chad. How are you?"

"Hi, Mrs. Taylor."

"Come in and sit those heavy bags down. So, what's the occasion?"

"Oh, I was a little homesick, and I wanted to come home for a few days," Zaria said.

"What about school? Aren't you guys missing classes?"

"No, classes are canceled for today and tomorrow. Saturday is our big game, and they're preparing the campus for tomorrow's pep rally.

"And you two are missing that?"

"Yeah, if you saw our pep rallies, you'd know we aren't missing much. My high school pep rallies were better than theirs," Chad answered.

"Oh, excuse me. I was just finishing up dinner. You're welcome to join us, Chad."

"Thanks, Mrs. Taylor. I think I will."

"Okay, good. Zaria, your brothers are upstairs. Why don't you two go up and say hello? I'll call you all when dinner's ready."

"Okay, Mom," she said as she grabbed Chad's hand and headed upstairs to see her brothers.

Something's not right, Shania thought to herself. It's strange for them to just show up here out of the blue without calling anyone. Something's fishy. The only time Zaria was home, when it wasn't during a break, was after Zach and Granny died. She sure has been acting strange lately, especially the last time she was here. Jesus, I pray that everything is all right with her.

She heard laughing and jostling coming from upstairs. The boys are probably just as surprised to see their sister as I am, Shania thought as she took a deep breath. If there's anything happening out of the ordinary, Trey will know. He's been Johnny on the case ever since he's been home, she smiled to herself.

Twenty minutes later, Shania called everyone for dinner. During dinner, as always, Trey was the first to break the silence.

"So, Chad, this is your last year, right?" he asked as he reached for the garlic bread.

"Yeah," Chad answered without looking up from his plate of spaghetti and sausages.

"So, what do you plan on doing once you graduate?"

"I don't know. I was thinking of taking some time off before I go to law school."

"Why would you do that, man?" Trey asked.

"I'm not sure; Zaria and I were thinking."

"Why are you questioning him?" Zaria snapped, cutting Chad off. "You're not his father."

"I'm just making small talk, Zaria," Trey responded.

"It sounds more like you're interrogating him to me."

"I can't ask the man about his future?"

"No. Mind your own business. Look how long it took for you to figure out what you wanted to do. If it wasn't for Grandpa Ray, you still wouldn't know."

"Okay, you two. We have a guest," Shania said.

"She started it. I was talking to Chad, not her," Trey replied.

"If you're talking to Chad, then you're talking to me," Zaria replied.

"Oh, so you two are one now?"

"Yes, we're soulmates. Tell him, Chad."

"That's enough, both of you. Zaria, there's nothing wrong with Trey asking Chad about his plans for the future," Shania said.

Just then, Chad stood up. "I have to get going. Thanks for dinner, Mrs. Taylor."

"You're leaving already? You haven't finished your dinner."

"I have to go. My parents are expecting me," he replied before grabbing his bag.

"So, your parents knew that you were coming into town?" she asked, looking at Zaria.

"No, I called them from upstairs to let them know I was here," Chad answered.

"Come on, Chad; I'll walk you to the door," Zaria said as she took his arm and walked out of the dining room.

When she returned, she picked up her and Chad's plates from the table.

"You're not going to finish eating your dinner, Zaria?" Shania asked, annoyed at her behavior.

"I lost my appetite," she said as she looked at Trey and rolled her eyes before walking out of the room.

"Zaria's been acting weird lately," Zane commented.

Someone else noticed that Zaria had been acting strange. Finally, Shania thought. She figured Trey would have been the one to notice Zaria's strange behavior first. Shaina was glad to know she wasn't the only one.

"She's acting just like a woman, temperamental," Trey said.

"Temper who?" replied Zane.

"Don't start with that stereotypical attitude, okay, Trey?" Shania replied as she got up from the table. "When you two finish eating, clean up the table, put the dishes in the dishwasher, and put the food that's left in containers before putting it in the fridge."

"Aww, come on, Mom. That's not fair," Trey said.

"No, it's not fair; it's just me being temperamental."

"What does temperamental mean?" Zane asked again.

"Look it up, Zane. And don't forget to turn on the dishwasher," she said.

The next morning, Zaria was up and dressed. She was drinking a glass of orange juice by the time Shania came downstairs.

"Where're you going so early this morning, Zaria?" Shania asked, surprised to see her up so early.

"I'm going to have breakfast with Chad and his family. Then we're going shopping."

"Okay, enjoy."

Later that evening, as Shania and the boys were cleaning up the kitchen, Zaria and Chad returned from shopping. After they put their bags in Zaria's room, they came into the kitchen as Shania was putting dishes into the dishwasher.

"Mom, can Chad and I talk to you in the family room?"

"Sure, baby. You boys finish up in here while I talk with your sister," Shania said as she left the room.

Trey and Zane looked at one another. Trey put his finger to his lips. He waited for them to go into the family room, and then he waved to Zane. They tiptoed and stood outside the family room to listen.

"So, what's up, you two?" she asked as she dried her hands on her apron.

"Mom, I'm pregnant."

"Oh no. Zaria, please don't tell me that."

162

"I'm sorry, Mom," she replied.

"Oh God, please don't let this be true. I can't take no more. What are you going to do?"

"What do you mean? What am I going to do? I'm going to have my baby."

"You're in your junior year of college, Zaria; you can't quit now."

"This semester is almost over, so I'm going to finish out the year. Then I'm going to transfer here and finish up my last year."

"What about your scholarship, Zaria?"

"I don't know. I get good grades. Maybe I can transfer my scholarship."

"And what if you can't? What do you plan on doing when the baby arrives?" Shania asked, looking at Chad.

"I graduate this year, so I'll take a year off and watch the baby while Zaria finishes school," Chad answered.

"Didn't you get accepted to law school?"

"Yes, but I can put it off for a year before going."

"Do you think that's wise, Chad?"

Chad looked down and shrugged his shoulders.

"What will your parents say?"

"We told them this morning. They're not happy."

"I'm sure. What do they think about your plans?"

"My father's a minister, so he wants us to get married before the baby's born. And he wants me to go to Law School. They said that they'd help with the baby.

"Married? Listen, I'm not too happy with the situation either. But the sin is not having a baby out of wedlock. The sinning happened long before that. That's something between the two of you and God. I think it would be wise for you and Zaria to complete your education before getting married. You can get married if you still feel the same way after you're finished."

"Chad's parents don't want us to wait."

"And your mother doesn't think you should get married now."

"May I ask why, Mrs. Taylor?"

"First of all, I don't think either one of you is ready for marriage."

"No disrespect, Mom, but don't you think that's up to us to decide?"

"Look, Chad asked me a question, and I'm answering it honestly, okay? You two never talked about getting married before this. Am I right?"

"Yes, you're right," Chad answered.

"I don't think it's wise for you two to get married now and put off your education because there's a good chance that you won't complete it."

"Mom, you're not listening. We said that I would finish this semester, take one semester off, and then go back and finish."

"Chad also said that he is going to put off going to law school to watch the baby while you're in school."

"What other choice do we have, Mom? I'm not getting an abortion."

Zane was hopping around on one foot with his hand over his mouth as if he were afraid that he might say something. Trey punched at him and mouthed for him to calm down.

"Did you hear me say anything about an abortion, Zaria? I'm talking about you finishing school before getting married. There are a lot of options out there. After the baby is born, we can look into putting the baby into family daycare for a few hours a day while you go to school. Or you can even take classes in the evenings. Chad's parents and I could help with the baby while you finish school.

"I don't know, Mom."

"Look, I need time to digest all of this. In the meantime, I want you to think about your life and where you want to be five years from now. I'm going to take this to God, and you two may want to do the same."

"Okay, but this is Chad's and my problem, and it's up to us to decide what we're going to do."

The boys ran back into the kitchen before anyone could see them. After walking Chad to the door, Zaria walked past the family room on her way to the kitchen.

"Zaria, can you come in here, please?"

"Mom, is this going to take long? Because I'm tired, and I want to get in my bed," she replied as she walked into the room, clearly trying to avoid her.

"No, this won't take long. First of all, this is not only you and Chad's problem. As long as you're living under my roof, it's also my problem. Now, I heard what Chad's parents want you all to do, and I heard what Chad wants to do. I've also told you what I think. What I haven't heard is what you want to do."

"Well, Chad and I thought…."

"I don't want to hear about what you and Chad think. I want to know what you, Zaria, want to do with your life and about this baby."

"Well, I want to have it, of course."

And? What are your plans? What do you want to do after you have the baby?"

"I definitely want to finish school. Eventually, I want to open my own psychotherapy practice."

"Okay. That's going to require a master's degree. How do you propose to do that while Chad goes to Law School?"

"His parents said that they would help us, she answered.

"You know, once you get married and have children, things will change. It's no longer about you. There are times when you'll have to sacrifice your needs and put not only your child's needs above your own but your husband's needs as well."

"I'm going to have to do that anyway once I have this baby."

"Yes, as far as the child is concerned, you will. You're at the prime of your life right now, Zaria; you should be pursuing your dreams and going after what you want."

"That's what I plan on doing, Mom, pursuing my dreams whether I get married or not."

"Once you get married, it becomes harder to finish your education. Often, it's the women who must put their dreams on hold."

"I know, but I've come too far for me to think about giving up."

"That's what I'm talking about. So, you'll take a little detour, but that doesn't mean you won't get to where you want to go. It will take some re-planning; it may even take a little longer, but you can still get back on track."

"That's exactly what I plan on doing."

"Okay. I know you're tired, so go on to bed, but I want you to take some time alone and think about your life and where you want to go from here."

"Okay, Mom," Zaria answered as she leaned over and kissed her mother. "Good Night."

She went into the den and poured herself a glass of Harvey's Bristol Cream over ice while Trey and Zane watched her from the kitchen. Zane shared his concern about his mother's drinking with Trey. Trey tried to assure him that it was only a phase and nothing to worry about.

A month after Zaria dropped the bombshell that she was pregnant, Trey told Shania that he decided not to join the Air Force. Although Shania had been angry with God ever since Granny's death, she thanked him for answering her prayers about Trey. If she learned nothing else, she learned that prayer works.

Trey said he was enjoying working with Ray, and he planned to continue doing this for a while since Ray offered him a permanent position. What he didn't tell her was that he wasn't going into the Air Force because he was afraid that his leaving might push her over the edge. She had not been herself since Granny died. She didn't sleep much, and she paced the floors at all times of the night. She was never much of a drinker, but after Cassandra left, she began to drink as soon as she got home on Friday evenings. She even stopped going to the Women's Ministry on Saturday afternoons with Lydia. He was glad that she still attended Church on Sunday.

They noticed that lately, the first thing she did when faced with difficulty was to reach for her Harvey's or a bottle of wine.

Zane would comment on her drinking to no avail, but as the oldest child, Trey felt that it was his responsibility to talk to her and to look out for her. After some discussion, he and Zane decided to speak with her together.

"Mom, Zane, and I want to talk to you about your drinking," Trey said as they walked into the living room, where Shania was sitting on the sofa, studying the bible on her lap while drinking a glass of wine.

"My drinking?"

"Yeah, look at you; you're drinking now while reading your Bible. What's that?" Zane said.

Trey held his hand up to quiet Zane; then he said, "We noticed that you've been drinking more than usual lately, and we're worried about you," trying to sound like the man around the house.

"There's no need to worry about me. Sometimes I like to have a drink on Friday evenings or after a long day at work. What's the big deal? You're acting like I'm an alcoholic or something."

"Drinking every Friday can become a problem, Mom. There is such a thing as weekend alcoholics, you know." Trey said.

"Yeah, besides, you have never drunk before. It wasn't until after Granny died and Aunt Cassy came that you started drinking," Zane interjected.

"We're just concerned about you. You've been through a lot lately, and now you have to deal with Zaria's situation," Trey said.

"Thanks for your concern, but I'm a grown woman, and I can take care of myself."

"We know you can," Trey replied.

"If my having a drink every once in a while, is bothering you guys, then I won't have one. It's not like I need to drink."

"It's not the once in a while that worries us, Mom," Zane said, "How come you started drinking after Granny died? You didn't drink like that after Dad died. Did Granny's death affect you more than Dad did?" Zane wanted to know.

What Zane hadn't realized was that Shania's way of handling Zach's death was by locking herself up in their guest room until Granny intervened.

"As for your father, our relationship was different from my relationship with Granny. Granny became a mother to me when I was eight years old. She was there for me through all the important events in my life, from the death of my mother to my marriage to the birth of my children right up to your father's death. So yes, her death had a greater impact on me, but her death has nothing to do with my drinking."

"If you say so," Zane pelted.

"For the record, Mr. Smarty Pants, there were many times after your father died that I wanted to have a drink, a smoke, or whatever.

However, I refrained from doing so because I was afraid that I would become dependent on it to ease my pain. God is all I need to depend on. So, if my having a drink on occasion bothers you, which it obviously does, then I won't do it. Okay?"

"Okay, Mom," Trey replied as he took hold of Zane's arm and led him out of the room before he could say anything more.

After the boys went back upstairs, Shania sat there for a while, thinking about what had just occurred. She realized that she, in fact, did begin to drink a little more after Granny died. What she hadn't realized was that the kids had noticed, too. Then, she picked up her glass and the bottle that she was drinking from, went into the kitchen, and poured what was left down the drain. She went back into the living room, picked up her Bible, held it to her chest, and asked God to give her the strength to get through the loss. Granny's death had hit her hard, and on some days, she didn't know how she was going to make it. On top of that, she broke into tears every time she allowed herself to think about Zaria. It was Granny's strength that got Shania through difficult times like these. She needed her now.

Shania decided that it was time to heed Granny's advice, get her mind off her own problems, and help someone else solve theirs. She took some time to think about what she enjoyed doing most in life.

A few weeks later, she submitted a proposal to the church for a new outreach program that focused on helping young people overcome depression. Shania wanted to offer some kind of intervention before they started to exhibit negative behaviors, which could lead to suicide.

After some discussion and planning, Tricia and Jake took it to the board, where it was approved. They even allowed Shania to hire a small staff of professionals to work with her and the youngsters. The program was so successful that they were able to get Government funding.

In the process of working with young adults with depression, Shania heard all kinds of stories, from neglect to sexual and physical abuse to the mental effects of having parents suffering from depression. All the things that lead to despair. Her heart felt heavy as she listened to their stories. She did her best to let them know that God loved them regardless of what they were going through.

She put together a mental health awareness program. From time to time, she had speakers come to speak with them as well as distribute inspirational books and materials. They had various professionals come in to work with them on the most crucial issues.

At one event, Shania told them about Zach's suicide and the hardships he faced in life. She told them that she believed if Zach had taken his fears to God, he would be here today. She wanted them to know that God was bigger than anything we could possibly face in life.

Chapter Nine
Time To Let Go

Shania realized that it was finally time to let go of all of Zach's belongings. It's been over three years, and she was finally able to make the decision once and for all to clear out his things. She had previously allowed the kids to go through his jewelry and take what they wanted. The boys spilt most of his jewelry amongst themselves except for his wedding band, which, of course, she kept along with his Rolex watch that she planned on giving to Zane when he graduated college. Zaria took his large gold chain with the letter 'Z.' Shania returned Zach's father's military medals and his Purple Heart to his mother, Ella.

Trey was excited to discover all of Zach's Jazz albums and CDs, which, he listened to non-stop. Although Shania had access to Zach's password and logins for his computer, she didn't use them, nor would she allow anyone else to, because she was afraid of what they might find.

With a new addition coming soon, now was the perfect time to get rid of Zach's things, which were just taking up space. She decided it was time to donate his clothes to the Salvation Army. So, she set aside her weekends to go through everything. While going through his dresser drawers, Shania noticed an envelope taped to the bottom of a drawer. Her face became flushed as she pulled the envelope down. It was sealed and addressed to her in Zach's handwriting. Seeing his handwriting made her excited and fearful all at once. She carefully opened the envelope. Her heart jumped when she noticed that it was dated the same day he died. She took a deep breath before reading it.

October 27, 2010

My Beloved Shania:

I knew, as thorough as you are that you would find this letter. First, let me express how sorry I am for all the hurt and pain my decision has caused you and the kids. My intentions were never to hurt anyone, especially not you, my love. You were the only constant thing in my life. Nothing brought me more joy than loving you and having you in my life for all these years. You and the kids have always been my only bright spot. It's just that that bright spot was not enough. I needed to know who I was and where I came from in order to know why I feel and act the way I do. I needed to know where my constant pain was coming from, so I began doing research to find out about my birth parents. Unfortunately, I found out.

I always knew the name of my birth mother since it's listed on my birth certificate. So, I began to research her people. I discovered that she had passed away. Her death certificate said that she died of mysterious circumstances. This piqued my curiosity, so I researched her family and found that most of them had also passed away. However, I did find their last known address here in Atlanta and discovered that her younger sister, Laura Simpson, still lives there. I reached out to her, and she agreed to meet with me. Laura told me all I needed to know about my birth parents, and it wasn't pretty.

The information I learned was too much for me to bear. I can't live knowing what I learned. I ask you, my love, to please understand my position and don't judge me too harshly. What I discovered is too much to put into this letter, but you will find all you need to know in a black box on the top shelf in the back of my closet. It is my hope that after you open the box, you will understand my pain.

Shania, you are a very special lady who deserves happiness, which is something I was unable to give you and have been unable to give you for some time. My hope is for you to find someone who will give you all the happiness and love that you deserve. I pray that you find it in your heart to forgive me so that you can go on with your life without me. Stay strong, my love, until we meet again.

Forever your Teddy Bear

Zachary A. Taylor, Jr.

Shania sat on the floor next to his dresser with the letter in her hand for what seemed like an eternity as the tears flowed down her face. "Wow", she said. "If only you had shared what you discovered with me, maybe we could have gotten through this together. It's so like you to keep your feelings bottled up and then act on them impulsively. It breaks my heart to think that you didn't trust me enough to tell me any of this in person."

She stood up and put Zach's letter to her nose to see if it held his scent before folding it and placing it on the dresser. Seeing Zach's handwriting brought on a new wave of emotions. She realized that it was fear as she walked over to her closet and grabbed the step stool inside. She kept repeating out loud, "I can do this, I can do this." As she climbed up the stool inside his closet. "Oh God, how I wish Granny was here," She thought. "I sure could use her strength right about now.'

She found the black box where Zach said it would be. She took it down, walked over to her vanity table, and proceeded to open it. Inside the box were neat but separate stacks of papers. One stack was copies of Zach's birth certificate and his adoption papers, as well as letters written to the Georgia State Adoption Board from Louise Simpson asking to resend the adoption request. In the letters, she stated that the request was fraudulent since the adoption papers were signed by her father, Louis Simpson. She stated that since she was legally an adult and was of stable mind, the adoption should not stand.

There was a letter from the Adoption Board turning down her request, stating that although she was considered an adult, she was unemployed and living under her father's roof. Therefore, she was deemed unfit and unable to care for an infant child. Notwithstanding, she was not married to the child's father or otherwise.

One stack held articles about Senator Louis Simpson, from his time as pastor to his three terms as a Georgia State Senator. In another neat stack were articles about the untimely and unsolved death of his oldest daughter, Louise Simpson, which led to his running for office. Last were clippings of his obituary. There was also a small black phonebook listing the addresses and telephone numbers of the late Senator's daughter, Laura Simpson, who lived in Atlanta, and the name and address of the nursing home for his wife, Anne Simpson.

Next, she found a manila envelope that read **Zach's notes on his findings**. In the envelope was a black composition notebook. She opened the notebook and began reading it.

January 4, 2007

My findings were told to me by Laura Simpson.

Birth mother, Louise Simpson, was born to a prominent family here in Atlanta. Her father was the late Senator Louis Simpson, who at one time was the pastor of the First AME Church in Atlanta. Her mother, Anne Boyd-Simpson, was the daughter of Marshall Boyd. He was one of the most successful black business owners in Atlanta. Anne Boyd-Simpson is now in her nineties and currently resides at Pinehill Nursing Home in Conveyers, GA.

Their birth father, John O'Connor, was an Irish man from the Boston area. He and Louise met during an anti-Vietnam war protest in Washington, DC. While there, they had a brief affair. A few months before returning to Atlanta, Louise learned that she was pregnant. She told John before he left to return to Boston. He had plans to attend theology school in the fall to become a priest. Realizing that this could ruin his family's high aspirations for him, John pleaded with her to have an abortion. Keep in mind that this was before Roe V. Wade, so a legal abortion was not a possibility. Since abortions were illegal at the time, John made plans for her to see an underground doctor in D.C., but Louise refused.

When Louise's parents learned of her pregnancy, they were appalled. Her parents went out of their way to keep her pregnancy hidden and made arrangements for her to put the baby (me) up for adoption. She had a change of heart and decided that she wanted to keep me. She made every attempt to retract the adoption. Nevertheless, the adoption went through.

According to Laura, Louise swore that she would do everything possible to get her child back, even if it meant going public. Her parents, afraid of ruining their family's good name, reached out to John O'Connor and asked him to speak with her in hopes of persuading her to let things be.

John told them that he was scheduled to be in Atlanta that next day and that he would meet and talk with her. Two days later, she was found in an alley, beaten within an inch of her life, barely holding on. She was rushed to the hospital; however, the doctors were unable to save her.

The Simpsons immediately reached out to John to find out what happened to their daughter, knowing that he must have been the last person to see her. However, he claimed that he never made it to Atlanta.

Although the Simpsons felt in their hearts that John was responsible for Louise's death, they didn't pursue it. They were afraid that the secret of Louise's illegitimate baby would get out. Needless to say, no one was ever charged with her death.

Louis Simpson used the unsolved death of his daughter as his platform to run for Senator. Suggesting that her death was not properly investigated, which in her case, like many negroes at the time, was not.

What her sister told me next rocked me to my core. Her father, Pastor Simpson, was one of two negroes running for a Senate seat in Georgia. It was important for potential elected officials and their families to be squeaky clean and beyond reproach, especially if they were colored. So, when he found out that Louise was pregnant with a white man's baby, he was beyond controllable.

This, of course, was in the late 1960s, a few months after the Supreme Court made interracial marriage legal in the US. However, Georgia repealed it, making interracial marriage illegal in the state until 1972. Due to Louis' standing in his church, having a baby out of wedlock was out of the question. So, you can imagine his fear, as well as the rage he displayed when Louise told him that she would stop at nothing to get her son back.

Now, I'm not saying whether he did something to her or not; what I'm saying is that the next day, he received word that Louise had written a letter to the adoption agency, asking to dissolve the adoption. Now, mind you, Louise was almost twenty, which, by all accounts, she was considered an adult. Upon hearing this, Louis stormed out of the house to go and talk some sense into her down at her job. When he got there, he was told that she had already left. He ran out of there on a mission to find her. What happened next is anyone's guess. All I know is that he came home some hours later, drenched in sweat and blood, with his clothes all wrinkled. He claimed that he searched all over town and couldn't find her. The next morning, someone knocked on our door and informed us that she was found beaten to a pulp in a nearby alley. She died a few hours later.

A few pages into the book, she found a written insert for her.

Shania, every time I think of the possibility that either my birth father or my grandfather was capable of such a horrendous act, I can barely look at myself. Knowing that I may come from such awful beings who can't possibly be human. I fear that when I go into my dark place, which I so often do, I don't know what I'm capable of doing. Am I the same as these awful people? The possibility of this makes it unbearable for me to go on.

Shania read all she could handle for one day. She put all the documents back into the black box except for the black telephone book. She pushed the box under her bed, and then she laid across it and began to weep. She cried for all the pain Zach had endured. She cried for all his birth mother went through, and most of all, she weeped for herself and her kids. She ended up crying herself to sleep.

When she awakened several hours later, she noticed that all the hurt she'd been feeling for the last three years began to lift. Her chest felt lighter. Somehow, she knew in her heart that she could no longer blame or fault Zach for his actions. Deep inside, she knew that from that moment on, she was going to be okay. She just wished Granny was here so she could share that moment with her. She finally had the closure that she needed. What she hadn't decided on was whether she was going to pursue what Zach had started and search for the truth or let it stay buried.

A couple of weeks later, after some deep thought, she decided to reach out to Laura Simpson to verify what she read in Zach's papers. She found her number and address in the telephone book that she found in Zach's black box. She called Laura, who said that she had been expecting her to call for a few years now. They agreed to meet the next day at Laura's home.

Laura greeted Shania with open arms as if they were old friends. Shania recognized her immediately. Maybe it was the family resemblance, she thought. Laura was not quite as fair as Zach was. However, they both had freckles and hazel-colored eyes. You could tell right away that they were kin.

Shania asked Laura what she meant when she said that she was expecting a call from her. Laura explained that Zach had reached out to her a year before his death, asking questions about his mother and their family. She invited him over, and she told him everything about his mother and the family.

"So, you knew about Zach's death?" Laura asked, surprised.

"Oh yes," Laura said, "his death made the newspapers. So sad, I even attended the funeral, but I stayed in the back."

"I do recall seeing you there. That's why you seem so familiar. You were in the back. Why didn't you say anything?" Shania asked.

"I didn't want to interfere. I figured that you would reach out to me in time."

Shania explained that although she knew that Zach was adopted, she had no idea that he had found her until she found his letter and the black box he left.

"I had no idea that Zach never mentioned our meetings. That explains a lot," Laura said.

"Zach had always been very private over the years. He usually managed to tell me what was happening, but he did so on his own time and in his own way. I guess his way of telling me about his family this time was through his suicide letter and the documents he left me in the box." Shania answered sadly.

"Well, that's an awful way to tell someone about your family, if you don't mind me saying so," Laura commented.

"Yes, it is. But knowing Zach, I'm not surprised. He always focused on the negative side of things. He never could see the brighter picture."

"Sounds like my daddy. Becoming a state senator was the worst thing that could have happened. He took on the problems of every black person in Atlanta. He tried to right all our problems during his time as senator, things we're still trying to make right to this day. When he saw that he couldn't change things, it ate him up inside. He would get so down and depressed that he wouldn't even talk to us. It got so bad he wouldn't even go into his Senate office. No matter how much Mama begged him to go and do what he was elected to do. He was too depressed to go in. He went down in history as 'Senator No Show.' Do you know how shameful that was for a Senator who went out of his way to help his people to be labeled 'Senator No Show'? I tell you, that was the beginning of his end. He died right there in that chair, staring out the window," Laura said as she pointed to a chair near a large window."

"Sounds like Zach, trying to take on the weight of the world."

"I could tell he was like my daddy in some ways. I even told him so."

"I read through the papers Zach gathered about his mother, but there's a lot I still don't understand. Do you mind clearing up a few things that you shared with Zach about your family for me? It may help fill in the blanks," Shania asked.

"Sure, baby, I'll be glad to tell you anything you want to know."

Shania went by Laura's home a few times, and she and Laura sat down over tea and some of Laura's homemade baked goods. Laura told her most of what Zach had written in his notes, which left Shania with a few questions of her own.

"Do you really think that your father was capable of killing his own daughter?" Shania asked.

"No, I don't," Laura answered. "You know, I saw the look in Zach's eyes when I told him how my father came home disheveled that evening, and I knew right there that I should not have told him. I've been keeping this for so long that I guess I had to share it with someone. Finally, seeing and talking with my big sister's son, whom I longed to meet, brought all of that out. I was disappointed with my Daddy in so many ways for so long, but I knew he didn't harm my sister."

"Why all the disappointment if he had nothing to do with it? Didn't he suffer her loss as well?" Shania asked, confused.

"Oh, I'm sure he did suffer, but he didn't show it, and he didn't want us to show it. I guess, to him, it was a sign of weakness. I was disappointed because he used her death as a way to get elected, and at the same time, he forbade us from talking about her at home. I always believed that he was fixated on becoming a senator more than he was on finding out what had happened to her. By telling Zach all of this was my way of letting go." Laura said with tears in her eyes. "I never imagined that my telling him this would put him over the edge."

"Please don't take this on. Zach's been through a lot in his life. Believe me, he had a multitude of issues long before he sat down with you." Shania explained.

"Do you think that his biological father had anything to do with Louise's death?"

"I really don't know. My father believed he did, but John claimed that he was never in Atlanta that day. We did learn, however, that he had a cousin who lived up in Roswell. When they sent someone there to question him, he refused to talk. You know the death of one of us didn't mean much back there, still don't."

"What happened to John? Is he still living in Boston?" Shania asked.

"No, child. John's long gone. He never did become a priest. Loved the women too much. Been married two or three times, from what I hear."

"Do you want to pursue this case and track down everyone that you think was involved?

"Oh no. Anyone who knew about this case is dead by now. All I ever wanted was to find Louise's son, and he found me. I'm just sorry that I didn't get to know Zach more or spend more time with him."

"Well, I would love for you to meet his children. We have one daughter, Zaria, who looks just like him, and two boys, Trey and Zane."

"Oh, I would love to," Laura answered.

"How about you come over for dinner on Sunday? I'll swing by and pick you up."

"Sounds like a date." Laura smiled.

This was the beginning of a wonderful journey for both Shania and Laura.

It's been four years since Zach's tragic death and two since Granny died. The Taylor family has been through a lot, but by the grace of God, they pulled through.

"Finally, good things began to happen for us," Shania thought. "We are finally on the other side of our pain." What she hadn't realized was that good things had been happening for them for a while now. She just didn't open her eyes or her heart enough to notice it.

Trey, who's been working at Ray's car dealership for almost two years, seemed happier than he's been in his entire life. He finally found his purpose. He was over the top with excitement when Ray asked him to come up with some ideas on how to attract younger customers. Trey was up for the challenge. He put together a plan and came up with a proposal that he presented to Ray. Atlanta had a lot of professional young people fresh out of college. A lot of them were from well-to-do families. They weren't into buying old cars, yet they were unable to afford a brand-new car right off the lot. He suggested they make some kind of deal with Cadillac and other luxury car dealerships to purchase one or two-year-old cars directly from them and resell the cars for a profit. They can also purchase high-end cars from rental companies like Hertz or Enterprise during their annual car sale and resell them at a slightly higher price for a profit. These cars will appeal to both the younger and the older, mature crowds. Ray liked the idea and decided to give Trey's theory a try. They began by purchasing year-old cars from Hertz's yearly restock sale and resold them for a small profit. Next, he did the same for Enterprise Rental Company. Then, they drafted a proposal and presented it to a local Cadillac dealership in the area to purchase any year-old cars that they were unable to sell for a reduced price. Cadillac accepted the offer, and they were able to flip the cars and make a profit. Trey's strategy worked so well that Ray rebranded his business and renamed it 'Ray and Trey's Used Luxury Cars.' Ray and Trey's used car dealership eventually became one of the most popular used car dealerships in Atlanta. As a reward, he offered Trey a percentage of his business, with the possibility of buying him out in the future.

Zaria and Chad decided that he would attend Law School in Texas while Zaria moved back home to complete her undergraduate degree. That following April, Zaria gave birth to a beautiful, healthy baby girl named Zequoia Juanita Taylor-Smith.

After taking a few months off to care for her newborn, Zaria went back to school for her master's degree while also working part-time. Shania pitched in by watching her granddaughter in the evenings and weekends while Zaria worked towards her goal.

Zane graduated from school at the top of his class. He received a full scholarship to Lincoln University in Virginia, where he studied Theology and Ministerial Studies. His goal was to become a pastor and open one of the largest churches in the state of Georgia.

Although things were going well for the Taylor family, Shania was becoming a little restless. Ever since her grandmother died, she felt a sense of uncertainty in her life. Her way of dealing with this was by trying to correct everything that she felt was wrong in her world. During the last year, since she and Laura became close, she recognized an underlying sadness in Laura. A sadness that she had once seen in Zach many times. When she asked her about it, Laura stated that her sadness came from her not knowing what happened to her sister. She hoped to get answers before she and her mother closed their eyes for good. Shania promised her that she would not stop searching for an answer to Louise's mysterious death until she found out what really happened to her.